THE CANAL
Lee Rourke

Melville House
Brooklyn, New York • London

The Canal

Second Melville House Printing: October 2010

Melville House Publishing
145 Plymouth Street
Brooklyn, New York 11201

and

Unit 3 Olympia Trading Estate
Coburg Road
London, N22 6TZ

mhpbooks.com

ISBN: 978-1-935554-01-1

Library of Congress Cataloging-in-Publication Data

Rourke, Lee.
The canal / Lee Rourke.
   p. cm.
  ISBN 978-1-935554-01-1
  1. Islington (London, England)—Fiction. 2. Psychological fiction. 3. Experi-
  mental fiction. I. Title.
PR6118.O885C36 2010
823'.92—dc22   2010011960

For Holly Ahern
I am atomised with you

We are suspended in dread.
Martin Heidegger

- PROLOGUE -

I started walking to the canal one day out of boredom. It's not that I'm particularly fond of canals; I don't give them much thought usually. I simply awoke one morning and decided, rather than walk to work as normal I'd walk to the canal instead. It was something about the light. I'd say it was almost crepuscular, even though it was some time between 8:30 and 9:00 in the morning and light can't be described as *crepuscular* at that time of the day. But to me, on that particular morning at least, it could.

Some people think that boredom is a bad thing, that it should be avoided, that we should fill our lives with other stuff in order to keep it at bay. I don't. I think boredom is a good thing: it shapes us; it moves us. Boredom is powerful. It should never be avoided. In fact, I think boredom should be embraced. It is the power of everyday boredom that compels people to do things—even if that something is nothing.

PART ONE
- boredom -

- one -

Along the towpath of the canal, halfway between Hackney
and Islington, I stopped at a brown bench. It was nestled
between two large hedges that had long since overgrown.
The towpath was busy with people walking and cycling
towards Islington on their way to work. Although I could
pretty much see everything from the bench, it was hard for
passers-by to see me until they were almost in front of me. It
was the perfect spot for me to sit, undisturbed; somewhere
I could do nothing and simply watch it all go by. The air
was still, silent—I could smell the water. It made me think
of the dredgers I used to watch as a child, the hard work
they did cleansing the bed of the canal. Behind the bench
was the exterior wall of a health centre used by the Packington Road Estate tenants. To the immediate left of this
wall, if I faced forwards towards the murky canal, was a
rusting iron bridge spray-painted in graffiti—the kind of
graffiti the perpetrators must have had to defy gravity to
apply—near a new-ish sign that read: Shepherdess Walk. A
tangle of iron railings and fences guarded the bridge from
people who thought it might have been a good idea to hurl
themselves off it into the canal—probably to spare them

from embarrassment, as the drop into the canal wouldn't lead to their deaths due to it being too short. Below the bridge, on a cemented-smooth stanchion was some original Banksy artwork that had been there a long time: a stencilled negative image of a man in a hood rolling a cigarette, or, more likely, a joint. It looked sinister, it looked real, it gave me the shivers—but I guess that's the point of urban graffiti. Above the bench, on the brick wall, yet more graffiti had been spray-painted up. This time in large silver letters which I had difficulty reading. I could make out: *312 Smar . . .*, but the three or four other letters that remained were gobble-degook. I tried to think what the word could be but gave up after about five minutes. I looked away, towards the direction of my tired feet resting in the worn-out patch of dirt and discarded cigarette ends below the bench. They reminded me of decorations sprinkled on top of a chocolate cake. In my peripheral vision I noticed, down next to my right thigh, etched into the brown panel of the bench, the words: *Pack Crew*. At least I could read that. I guessed the Pack Crew belonged to the Packington Estate that stretched along the canal behind me. I turned to the murky water. I watched the Canada geese. Two of them. Mates. I liked them. I always have done. They've lived—various geese, the coots, the moorhens—on this canal for as far back as I can remember. They ignored me as they inspected a box that was floating beside them, before they stopped to preen each other and then took turns sifting the silty banks for titbits—arses to the world. I began to think about my childhood: I couldn't believe that I used to swim in this very canal—when the locks were full, the oil dripping from my ears, dodging the floating scum that had built up near the lock's edge. I thought nothing of the pollution back then.

On the other side of the bank stood a large whitewashed building that had probably been erected in the late eighties or early nineties. But I could be wrong; it could just have been renovated about that time. The building could be much older—maybe the 1930s. It probably is, come to think of it. It came right to the water's edge as the elegant buildings in Venice do, although this monstrosity was far from elegant. Green moss and damp had started to grow where the water lapped against its white façade, causing odd shapes and patterns along the entire water-side length of the building. To any passing eye these patterns could have easily been mistaken for trees and bushes growing directly out of the canal. But they weren't, of course—it was just general muck due to a lack of maintenance by the building's owners. Above this was a private esplanade formed entirely of grey concrete. From where I was sitting, if I stared straight ahead, I could clearly see that the building was split into two halves: the ground floor, by the esplanade, above the murky moss by the water's edge, was packed with rows of snazzy flat-screen monitors, each accompanied by an office worker—some on phones, some not. The five floors above this bustling office consisted of the goldfish-bowl-like abodes of the upwardly mobile. Record collections and bland modern art— colourful splodges of paint, or black and white iconic images—could be seen hanging from the white walls inside the large looming windows that seem to be the fashion with these buildings. Numerous balconies featuring self-assembled Ikea and Habitat tables and chairs jostled for position, and those affluent enough to be on the fifth floor had veiled themselves, and their lives, with arrays of foliage on each roof terrace.

It made me feel like smiling.

It was good sitting there, watching the world go by— saying nothing, doing nothing, thinking nothing. It was really good. I noticed that one office worker in particular, dressed in a light blue shirt and pink tie—both obviously expensive—kept getting up from his desk and walking over to another desk about ten to twelve times per hour. He looked stressed. He would stand at the other desk—a woman was sitting at it—for about three minutes, looking at her flat-screen monitor, and then he would traipse back to his own desk. I had been watching the two Canada geese that had been floating back and forth, constantly giving me the eye—like they were expecting me to feed them. Back and forth. Back and forth. Back and forth. The office worker in the blue shirt and pink tie would shoot off one way and the two Canada geese would paddle by in the opposite direction. Back and forth. Back and forth. Back and forth. Maybe ten or twelve times per hour. Maybe more. I think I stayed on the bench watching the two Canada geese, the man in the blue shirt and pink tie and his fellow office workers for three or four hours or so, I'm not sure. Just counting them, watching their repetitive movements. I probably would have stayed there all day if it wasn't for the old lady who had suddenly joined me. She reeked of urine and was in layers upon layers of clothing: cardigans, coats, tights, hats, body warmers, et cetera. She had no teeth, only a black hole for a mouth. She kept asking me over and over and over again in a slurred northeast London brogue.

"Do you like the canal, then? Do you like the canal, then? Do you like the canal, then? Do you like the canal, then? Do you like the canal, then? Do you like the canal, then? Do you like the canal, then? Do you like the canal, then? Do you like the canal, then? Do you like the canal, then? Do you like the canal, then? Do you like the canal, then? Do you like the canal, then?"

I didn't answer her the first time she had asked, so it struck me as odd that she would persist. I got up from the bench and left her without saying a word. I headed back towards Hackney. I was sure she was still asking the same question over and over and over again as I walked away.

I was hungry.

- two -

The very next day, instead of walking to work, I headed back to the bench. Before I got to my bench, I noticed a sign fixed to the railings along the walk-way up to the estate. It was a *British Waterways London* sign. An official *Towpath Code of Conduct*. Beneath this heading was a list of dos and don'ts. Some of them seemed quite petty, but on the whole, the sign seemed to make sense. Up on the wall, it looked quite threatening.

British Waterways London
Towpath Code of Conduct

Pedestrians have priority
Considerate cycling permitted
Give way at bridges
Be careful at bends & entrances

Cyclists:
Ring with two tings
Pass people slowly
Give people space

Pedestrians:
Listen for two tings
Allow people to pass

I found the word *tings* amusing. I decided to sit on the bench and see if any of the numerous cyclists that passed me by would adhere to the *two tings* rule. Most of the cyclists who passed me by, weaving in and out of those people walking along the towpath, ignored the rule and certainly didn't consider the well-being of those around them. And those who did *ting* their bells often *tinged* their bells more than four or five times, waiting until they were right up behind the pedestrian before doing this. This caused most pedestrians to jump; to get annoyed and mutter obscenities. It didn't take me long to observe that there was a lot of ill feeling between the cyclists and pedestrians: a sort of passive-aggressive turf warfare was in progress. I wasn't going to interfere.

The Canada geese were in full cry—as were the coots. I liked my spot across from the flat-screen monitors and superfluous balconies. I liked being bored—I liked what it was doing to me. The word "boring" is usually used to denote a lack of meaning—an acute emptiness. But the weight of boredom at that precise moment was almost overwhelming, it sure as hell wasn't empty of anything; it was tangible—*it had meaning*.

It was important for me to be sitting on that bench. I pondered this conclusion for about an hour or so. It felt good—so good, in fact, that I hadn't noticed the young woman who had joined me. I glanced to my right: blue. She was wearing blue. She had brown hair—medium-length and of no particular style. I caught a light whiff of her scent in the breeze: she smelt clean, as though she had just stepped out of the shower. She stared straight ahead, motionless, silent. I smiled.

Two hours later we were both still sitting on the bench. We hadn't even acknowledged each other—although it was obvious she was aware that I was aware of her. And then, suddenly, without making a sound, she got up from the bench and walked away, towards Hackney. I remember that this pleased me: Not the fact that she was walking away, but that she was heading back towards Hackney and not Islington. I hold a lot of ill-feeling towards Islington. It's not my kind of place—no matter how hard it tries. If I was an estate agent then maybe I would feel at home—but I'm not an estate agent.

- three -

Little by little, yet another pattern was beginning to emerge in my life. It was between 8:30 and 9:00 in the morning, and once again I was to be found sitting on the bench. This time I was fully aware when she arrived one hour or so later. I had spent the time waiting for her to arrive—not that I knew she would—thinking about the dredgers. They still hadn't visited this section of the canal, although they had been at work farther down towards Angel at the wharf, and scum and debris was beginning to fill up the stretch between the rusting iron bridge and the whitewashed office block. I had already counted twelve empty beer bottles float by, maybe ten or eleven crisp packets of various description, four or five bits of wood, one milk carton, and about sixteen plastic bottles. Scum was beginning to settle by the moss growing up the whitewashed building at the water's edge. Things were beginning to look a mess.

I wanted to see them, the dredgers. I wanted to see them in action. I wanted to see what they might find buried in the thick sludge. I got up off the bench and walked to the bank. I peered down. I couldn't even see my own reflection in the water—let alone what was down there, below the surface. I felt aggrieved by their no-show. I contemplated contacting

British Waterways London, or maybe Hackney or Islington council to see if an emergency dredger team could be deployed immediately. But I didn't own a mobile phone—I had thrown the last one I owned into the dustbin in disgust—so I was unable to phone for the number. I would have even paid the extra charge and demanded that I be put straight through. I walked back to the bench wondering what I could do with myself. I kicked my heels into the dirt, scattering the used cigarette ends, and moved them about, to make random patterns and then erased them, over and over again. I looked over at the snazzy flat-screen monitors. The same man I'd watched before—this time dressed in a slim-fitted white shirt and a thin blue tie—was walking back and forth, back and forth, back and forth. A lone coot trundled along in the canal below him, its large feet paddling like crazy against the current. The man in the slim-fitted white shirt and thin blue tie got up and walked towards the other desk in his office. He walked in the same direction as the coot on the canal, and for a fleeting moment they were both parallel with each other, heading in the same direction and at the same speed, until the coot stopped and dived to the bottom of the canal for something it had spotted.

I looked to my right as she walked over to sit down on the bench: black. She was dressed head to toe in black this time. Like the day before, she began to stare straight ahead. It was probably my discomfort over the dredger shirking its responsibility that caused me to stare at her longer than I, perhaps, should have done. I was pretty sure that she was aware of this, and I'm maybe sixty percent sure that I saw her eyes dart to her left for a nanosecond. But I could have been wrong—like most people I can be quite vainglorious at times. She could have been blinking.

It is obvious that boredom has existed since the dawn of man. I realise that this is quite a pompous statement—*the*

dawn of man—but I can think of no other way of express-
ing this, so the cliché will have to do. It has existed in
various forms, since before there was a word for it, since
long before the word *boredom* and its equivalents across the
globe sprang into existence. I often wonder how the feeling
of *boredom* was expressed before we had the language to
express it. We must have lazed about, much like a bored dog
does, making noises: huffing and puffing, sighing—things
like that. Eventually we would have begun to feel the same
urges we still find hard to articulate—it must have been a
very confusing time for us. I'm not sure that many people I
know have thought about this before, not because I think on
some deeper, more intellectual level—I don't. I've certainly
never discussed it with any of them. They'd probably find
the subject boring and want to talk about more interesting
things like sex and war, or terrorism.

I suppose I wanted her to look at me. I suppose I wanted
her to be interested in me like I was in her. But every time
I looked to my right she was still there, staring steadfastly
ahead—not even the faint glimmer of interest, it seemed.

- four -

It was a Friday afternoon. The very same commuters—I
could recognise their faces, their bikes, their suits—I had
seen that morning, shuffling into Islington and central London, were now making their way back, past the bench, under
the rusting iron bridge; past the Canada geese, the coots, the
moorhens, the whitewashed office block and trendy, lifeless
flats, back towards Hackney and its environs. She uttered
these words to me:

"Why do you come here everyday? You never used
to . . ."

My right leg began to shake; I didn't know what to say. I looked at her. She looked at me. I noticed that she had large dark eyes, a little droopy, cat-like, made up that way, the corners turned up with a flick of eye-liner—I was instantly attracted to them. To her. But this was nothing new, as I was often attracted to complete and utter strangers.

"Well?"

Her persistence unnerved me. I stammered. My right leg shook even more than usual.

"I . . . er . . . I'm bored."

That was all I managed to say to her because as soon as I said it she got up and walked away, back towards Hackney, with the rest of the commuters. My leg stopped its involuntary paroxysms. I stared at the office workers across the canal: one by one they switched off their flat-screen monitors. Some left the building alone, others in twos and threes—to begin the journey home, I guessed, or maybe to the nearest public house, it being a Friday. I got up and headed home towards Hackney as well.

- five -

A lot of people have attributed boredom to a lack of things to do—this has always confused me. For me the act of boredom, by its very nature, is doing something. As I have mentioned before, boredom moves me, it forces me to react. Boredom is often viewed as a defect of character, but this is wholly unfair. People who are bored are usually perceived by others as not willing to interact with those around them, or with society as a whole. This couldn't be further from the truth: those who are bored, and, more importantly, embrace their boredom, have a far clearer perspective on a) them-selves, and b) those around them. Those who are not bored are merely lost in superfluous activity: fashion, lifestyle, TV, drink, drugs, technology, et cetera—the usual things we use to pass the time. The irony being that they are just as bored as I am, only they think they're not because they are continually doing something. And what they are doing is battling boredom, which is a losing battle.

I spent the whole weekend with them, drinking in the same pub, with the same people, the same faces; drinking the same drinks, saying the same things. After I had exhausted myself saying the same things I simply said nothing. I let those around me say the very same things for me. I drank. I can't even remember stopping to eat, although I figure I must have done at some point. All I really wanted was to be back at the canal. My weekend was a waste. I wanted to be back on that bench, waiting for her.

- six -

It was Monday morning. The same commuters, the same bench. I didn't care about the time; it was starting to pass me by anyway. I was sitting, picking at a spot that had formed on the bridge of my nose. Picking at the skin, the slight swelling around it. Pushing it in; tracing the bump that had formed with the tip of my finger. Stubble had begun to grow on my face, spreading like a virus. I had stopped shaving, but not consciously—I'd forgotten that that's what I liked to do, that's all. I continued to pick at my spot on the bridge of my nose. It took me a while to work out what had caused it: a wine glass. Well, many wine glasses over the course of the weekend, aggravating the skin as the rim caught it each time I tilted my head back to finish another glass. After I had worked that out it didn't irritate me quite as much.

I found my thoughts drifting of their own accord towards her; I wanted her to turn up. I hoped that my crumbling riposte the previous week hadn't alarmed her.

I fell for a girl in my class at school. She was called Caitlin Booth. Her parents were from Dublin and she had lived there up until the age of ten. Her accent was beautiful and mellifluous. I used to sit behind her. I would ignore the teacher (to such an extent that I can no longer remember which lesson it was we were attending). I would look at her golden hair, nestling on her shoulders—occasionally she would flick it, or tilt her head to the right, letting it fall over her blue eyes. The skin on the back of her neck was pale, freckled, and her clothes smelled faintly of the chips she had eaten at lunchtime. To me she was beautiful. One day I was instructed to sit next to her when the teacher grouped us all into pairs to work together on some exercise or other. I could hardly breathe, I was that nervous. My leg was probably shaking more that it ever has—either that or it was then that it first began to happen. I watched her take her pencil case and books from her bag. I looked at her books: on the back of one she had scrawled, *Caitlin Booth loves Anthony Lomax 68%* and, *Caitlin Booth loves Aaron Maguire 54%* and, *Caitlin Booth loves Sean Owen 91%*. I could have died on the spot. She noticed me looking at her books; she smiled and asked me what I was looking at. So I told her. She told me that she didn't *really love them*, that it was just *a bit of fun.* Then she said she'd do it for me. She wrote down her name and then mine. Then she began a multiplication and subtraction routine based, it seemed, on the letters in our names and their place in the alphabet. I stared. But I soon noticed that instead of writing the word *loves* in between our names—like she had done with the other names scrawled on her book—she had replaced it with the word *loathes*. I had never heard this word before—let alone seen it written down. I remember asking her what it meant: she told me that *it was just another word for love*. It felt like my whole body was shaking. Soon the multiplication and subtraction was complete and she showed me the result: she loathed me 98%. I realise now that I have no idea or recollection as to what her true percentage was. I just remember being elated. That night, happy and madly in love, I looked up the word *loathes* in the pocket Oxford dictionary that I used to keep by my bed. I never looked at Caitlin Booth again.

I tried not to look bothered when she finally arrived: green. She was dressed in green. As usual she slowly sat herself down to my right. This time she turned directly towards me:
      "So, you're here again?"
      "Yes."
      "*Bored*?"
      "Yes."
      "I'm worried . . ."
      "Why?"
      "The dredgers haven't arrived . . ."
      "I've been thinking about that, too."
      "Are you just saying that?"
      "No, really, I've been waiting for the dredgers, too."
      She released a long, drawn-out yawn. It seemed to last aeons; the whole shape of her face changed. It reminded me of an Aphex Twin video I had once seen that I cannot recall the name of—not particularly being a fan of Aphex Twin's music. After she has finished yawning she turned to me again:
      "I once lied to my boyfriend . . ."
      "What about?"

"I told him that I was pregnant. I told him that it was his baby . . ."

"Wasn't it his baby?"

"It was no one's baby . . ."

"Eh?"

"It was no one's baby . . ."

"What do you mean?"

"There was no baby . . . That was the lie."

"What?"

"I wasn't pregnant . . . I told him that I didn't want it."

"The imaginary baby?"

"Yes."

"Okay."

"I told him that I wanted an abortion . . . *Immediately* . . . And, because he was the father, he should pay for it. That it, the baby, was as much his responsibility as mine . . ."

"Did he pay?"

"Yes. The whole amount. The last thing he wanted to be was a father."

"What did you do with the money?"

"I spent it on a weekend in the Lake District with my best friend. We got drunk, fucked men, had fun . . ."

"Why?"

"Why have fun?"

"No . . . Why lie to your boyfriend like that?"

"Because he deserved it. He was cheating on me. He didn't care about me. He hated me. Oh, the usual stuff, you know. The only thing he cared about was money, so I hit him where it hurt. In his pocket. Money was everything to him, still is probably, I don't know really. It was all he lived for. Money. Money. Money. Money. Money. It's all everyone lives for, it seems."

"I suppose you're right."

"I am right. I turned his guilt, his hatred for me into a commodity. And he—the moron—bought into it. He bought his own piece of me. And at the same time hated the fact that he had to give me, of all people, money. These are the depths people will sink to."

She began to pick at the skin near her fingernails. The skin looked smooth and shiny. She was fresh-looking and clean. She stared straight ahead, towards the office workers in the whitewashed building opposite. I watched her chest rise and fall. I didn't know what to say to her. A discarded can of beer floating by caught my attention. A lone swan avoided it, paying it no attention whatsoever.

We sat on the bench in silence for maybe an hour before I asked her.

"What's your name?"

"That doesn't matter."

"Why?"

"Because I prefer to remain anonymous."

"Why?"

"Things are easier like that . . . You'll see the end of me anyway"

"I think I know what you mean."

With this she got up to her feet and walked off towards Hackney. I watched her. I liked her gait. She walked with purpose, yet slowly, like she was floating, her head in the clouds, yet towards something, a confrontation, maybe. I stood up.

"Wait! Wait! Wait! Wait! Wait! Wait! Wait!"

Eventually she stopped, but she didn't turn around. I ran towards her; just as I got to her she turned to face me.

"What?"

"Er . . ."

"What?"

"Well . . . Will you be here tomorrow?"

"Yes . . . I always come by this way."

She continued on. I turned around and walked back to the bench. *"You'll see the end of me anyway . . ."* It stuck in my mind, even though I had no idea what she was talking about. I tried not to think about it too much. But it was hard not to.

I looked over at the office workers opposite, sitting at their snazzy monitors. It was like I'd never even had a job. I couldn't continue with that sort of thing anymore. Work was nothing to me now. I was happy—happy that I wasn't them, stuck in that dreadful place of work. I decided that I would go home and compose a letter of resignation. And I would write this letter in my own hand. An email wouldn't suffice; I wanted my letter to be authentic.

- seven -

Dear Richard,

I can't go on anymore with this. I can't see the point. I don't expect you to understand my feelings about this. I am bored with work full stop. Not your company, but work. You may think that I am ergophobic, that I need help, that there is an obvious solution to this—there isn't, Richard, not in the way you're thinking. I am simply bored. I am not sick. I have no psychological disorder. I simply want to embrace my boredom— and my boredom forces me to walk away from work.

Some people work because they are bored—they aren't aware of this fact though. Some people spend their entire working lives bored and never once question this. They accept this by trying to quell it; maybe they would be a lot happier if they tried embracing it rather than trying to ignore it—or battling against it—all their miserable/happy

*lives. I am embracing boredom—yes—that's what I am doing.
I don't need to clear my desk; those things are superfluous to
me now. Richard, I wish you every success in your venture.
No hard feelings, eh? Goodbye, talking about boredom bores
me. I must act.*

*Yours,
A happy man.*

- eight -

I was waiting for her when I was suddenly surrounded by a
group of teenagers. They just seemed to appear out from the
foliage or something. Two plonked themselves down either
side of me on the bench. The other two loitered threaten-
ingly in front of me, music blaring from a snazzy mobile
phone, blocking my view of the canal and the whitewashed
office block. The music they were listening to was Dizzee
Rascal—although it could have been any one of the numerous *grime* stars of London. Dizzee Rascal is the only one I
have heard of, so I presumed it was him. Then they began
to swap places. I found this very unnerving. A couple of
them began shouting along with the tinny music blaring
from the snazzy mobile phone. I started to feel uncomfortable, even though they were clearly much younger than
me. Two of them had put their hoods up (something I
usually liked; aesthetically, if done correctly, a group of
teenagers dressed this way can look striking). They began
to lean over me.
    "What you doing, man?"
    "What you up to, man?"
    "What you doing?"
    "What you doing here?"

This seemed to be ejaculated at once; a cacophony of teenagers and testosterone—a heady combination.

"What you doing on this bench for, man?"

"What you doing on this bench?"

"What you doing just sitting here?"

"What you doing, man?"

My right leg began to shake. I wanted to shout, to start running, but I couldn't muster the energy.

"Are you a battyboy, man?"

"Are you a battyboy, innit?"

"Are you a battyboy?"

"Battyboy, man?"

I looked across to the office workers through a gap between two of the teenagers. There must have been a meeting in progress at one of the desks, as all the staff had wheeled their chairs over to it. I counted ten in total, but it was hard to determine for certain as the two teenagers in front of me kept obstructing my view. I could see a woman addressing the team. All, except one who was looking directly over to me. He was young. I'm sure he was smiling.

"What you doing, man?"

"Do you suck wood, man?"

"Are you battyboy, innit?"

"Do you have any money, innit?"

It was rapidly turning into my worst nightmare. I had no money on my person. If I told them I had no money they would turn violent, that's how these situations unfold.

"Have you got any money, man?"

"Have you got any money?"

"You got money, man?"

"Have you got any, man?"

The smallest of the four—who had bright red hair— began to fumble for something inside his pockets. He yawned. He pulled out his cigarettes. I let out a sigh—I thought he was searching for a knife. I thought he was going to threaten me with it; it's always the smaller ones with something to prove. He lit his cigarette with a match and flicked the still-lit match at a lone coot on the canal, missing it by half a foot or so. I could smell the sulphur. He turned and exhaled the blue smoke into my face. He muttered something to the other three in slang that I couldn't understand. They laughed.

"What you here for then?"

"Yeah, what you doing here?"

"Looking for business?"

"Looking for some wood to suck?"

I looked up at the tallest of the four; he had a shaved head. He reminded me of an old school friend whom I hadn't thought about in over twenty years: Sean Murray, who used to spend all day and night on his computer, learning binary code and basic programming. It made no sense to me then as much as now: numbers and instruction. It's meaningless to me. Sean Murray wouldn't have hurt a fly. He still wouldn't. The teenager with the shaved head leaned closer to me.

"Why you here, we just asked you?"

"Why you here, man?"

"Man, why you here, innit?"

"Yeah man, why you on this bench?"

I jolted upright, my muscles tensing, fear gripping me.

"Because, I'm bored . . ."

The nanosecond of silence seemed to last aeons before the four teenagers collapsed into laughter.

"Let's leave this battyboy, man."

"Yeah, we can go up Mare Street."

"But he might have money, man."

"He ain't got no bean, man."

I watched them as they walked away, laughing, patting each other on the back, swaggering. They began to pick up stones and throw them into the canal. The red-haired teen-ager looked back at me and made some sort of hand/finger gesture, the kind I've seen used in gangster rap videos—it looked stupid used in this context, near the coots and Can-ada geese on the canal. I began to wonder if the teenagers were part of the Pack Crew I'd seen spray-painted around the area. Whoever they were, they were certainly intimidat-ing. I watched them as far as I could (which wasn't that far as the overgrown privets impeded my view), although I didn't try too hard, as I didn't want to look like I was star-ing at them. They may have seen this as a signal, they may have come back, and I didn't want that to happen.

My right leg soon stopped shaking. I looked at the reflec-tion of the whitewashed office block in the murky water, just a faint trace of it; the sun above had broken free from a heavy-looking cloud. The faint reflection shimmered and morphed into different shapes with the changing patterns of the murky water. I looked back up. The meeting was still in progress and the office worker who was once looking directly at me was now looking at some figures projected onto the far white wall of their section of the office via an overhead projector. The woman who seemed to be conduct-ing the meeting was struggling to use her laptop. The office workers present seemed to be staring up at the projected image regardless of her inability. Pretty soon the projected image on the white wall changed: it became a red and blue graph, the sort used for such a benign purpose. The woman must have cracked a joke about her inability to use the technology provided—this must've been the case because I've never seen one person laugh at a graph for no reason, let alone about ten people.

It was later than usual when she eventually arrived. I'd lost count of how long I'd been waiting—it must have been a long time, though, because the office workers, as they did each evening, had started to switch off their flat-screen monitors, and the pedestrians and cyclists on the towpath were now moving in the opposite direction as they were that morning.

She was wearing black and white. I had started to notice more about her. She always seemed so clean; flat shoes, tight trousers falling above her ankles. Her skin smooth and tender. She was unlike most people from that area; even the art students and young professionals didn't look quite like her. She was, or seemed, different. She sat closer to me than usual. She was smoking a cigarette—I hadn't noticed this about her before. I'm not the biggest fan of people who smoke. She started to speak to me immediately.

"You're here . . . ?"

"Yes."

"Were you waiting for me?"

"Yes."

"What have you been doing?"

"Some teenagers . . . from the estate . . . they started harassing me . . ."

"Oh."

"Yes, four of them. I thought they were going to mug me . . ."

"They come here a lot."

"Who do?"

"Teenagers do . . . There's nothing much for them to do . . . What did they look like?"

"Hoods. One of them had bright red hair."

"Yes."

"What?"

"They come here often. I know who you mean. It's their patch . . . their territory, it seems . . ."

"Their territory?"

"They're a gang. I presume they are. They're looking out."

"What for?"

"Other gangs . . . people to harass."

"Oh."

"What did they say to you?"

"They asked me if I was a homosexual . . ."

"Are you?"

"I didn't say anything. I think they wanted money. No, I'm not."

"There's nothing else for them to do. Money affords them the lifestyle they are told they need. They're just waiting . . ."

"Waiting?"

"To become adults."

"Waiting to become adults?"

"Yes. Adults, it's obvious . . . It's . . ."

She fell into silence as a woman walking a pet Staffordshire Bull Terrier ambled by the bench. The dog happily sniffing along. I watched the dog; it looked so happy. It actually looked like it had a smile on its face; sniffing around at stuff, litter, rubbish, and scraps of things, running from one bench to another, catching the scent left behind from other dogs—coded messages that were invisible to us humans. The owner looked to be in her mid-twenties. I don't know, though, she could have been younger. It was hard to tell. She was wearing sports gear—white Reebok trainers, grey jogging bottoms, a navy blue hooded top—as well as gold earrings and bracelets. Her clothes were too tight for her bulging arse and torso; her gut lolloped about. She had dyed blond hair, the roots dark; it was scraped back to such an alarming extent that she looked startled. Her face was heavily made-up. Her large earrings dangled, respondent to each of her aggressive movements.

She was screaming at the dog.

"Come here you little cunt. Come here. Don't go near those people. Come here you little cunt. Come here. Watch those fucking people. Come here you little cunt. Come here. Don't go too far. Come here. Come here you little cunt. Don't go near those two people. Cunt. Come here you little. cunt. Come here. Cunt. Come here you little cunt. Don't go near them. Come here."

The dog wandered over to me. It was a beautiful dog. Sandy brown. A bitch. She looked up at me and I petted her head and around her thick, muscular neck. She jumped up playfully and tried to lick my face.

"Come here you little cunt. Don't try to attack the man. Come here you little cunt. Come here. Leave the man alone. You little cunt. Leave the man alone. Come here."

I looked up.

"Really, it's no problem . . . She's a lovely . . ."

The dog ran back to her. She kicked the dog in the rib-cage. The dog yelped so loud it caused some coots to scatter across the murky water.

"That'll teach you to come here you little cunt."

The woman and the sandy dog walked away. The dog looked up at its owner, tail between its legs. I felt disgusted. I should have done something—at least said something to the owner.

I turned back to her sitting next to me.

"Did you see that?"

"Yes."

"That's disgusting. She doesn't deserve to own that beautiful dog."

"She comes by here all the time . . . Always the same, always so aggressive. We can only live in hope that one day the dog will come to its senses and fight back."

"Is that what you really think?"

"Yes, of course, all the time."

As she said these words, up above, an Airbus 310 travelling to Heathrow began to wind down. Its engines let out a howl that could be heard for miles around. I looked up: the plane was banking over the city; it was quite low in the sky, well below the thick cloud. It looked colossal, a massive floating machine. I momentarily thought of the twin towers, and where I was that day, but the image soon passed. I followed the plane's trajectory as it curved around the city, banking to its right, eventually straightening out to follow the route of the Thames westwards to the strip of reinforced concrete it was due to land on. Planes follow these same paths, to greater or lesser degrees, day and night, and no one bats an eye-lid, no one finds it at all remarkable. Often I would point out the moment the plane's engines could be heard winding down for the final approach to whomever I was with at the time. Most would utter *Oh* or *Yeah* but none would enthuse like me, none would see the beauty in this. I would point out the plane as it banked in the sky, but no one seemed interested. Sometimes when I looked up the plane seemed to be stationary, floating, hanging there in the sky, dangling with nothing to do, like a beautiful painting before me. Then I would look around to see if anyone else had noticed this and no one else would be looking up at it, everyone else would be in transit, oblivious, getting on with their business. No one was ever interested. They'd only be interested if the plane was hurtling towards oblivion or something—like that time in New York. Then everyone would stop and look. But it's still the same plane. It's still the same plane.

"I have a son."

"Pardon?"

She inched up the bench so that she was sitting beside me, our thighs nearly touching. A perfectly plucked eyebrow raised itself above her left eye. Something shot through me, like some sort of charge. I felt like a breakthrough had been made.

"I said I have a son.",

"Oh. I mean wow, that's great! Isn't it?"

"A son."

"What's his name?"

"That doesn't matter."

"How old is he?"

"Old enough to know that I'm his mother."

"So, why are you telling me this?"

"Because I don't love him?"

"What do you mean?"

"I mean that I wish he didn't exist, that I didn't fall pregnant with him, that I didn't give birth to him . . . That's what I mean. Like that lie I told you about. I wish it could all be forgotten about."

"Why don't you love him?"

"I don't know . . . All I know is that I feel nothing for him."

She leaned closer to me; she looked me in the eye. Her eyes tightened and wrinkles appeared around them like oyster shells. I noticed a faint mole on her cheek. Her lips were thick.

"You're the first person I've ever told."

"About you not feeling anything . . . ?"

"Yes."

"Does he know?"

"That I don't love him?"

"Yes . . ."

"I guess so . . . He's a bright lad. He's not stupid. There's a book out . . . Have you read it? It deals with . . ."

"No. I don't read that many books."

"Oh."

"Why are you telling me these things?"

"Because I don't know you . . . I find it easier to talk to strangers, real strangers, not some pathetic voice on the end of a phone. Unlike my friends, the few I have, I don't care what you think about me."

"Do you feel you've got a lot to talk about?"

"No more than everyone else . . . I don't know. I just feel like talking."

"That's fine by me . . ."

"I know."

"*You know*?"

"Yes. I could tell that you would listen. Plus, bored people will listen to just about anything."

"Right . . . How do you know I'm bored?"

"You *told* me."

"Right."

We both stopped to watch a narrow boat pass us by. It was called *Angel*. It was probably the smallest I had ever seen. I remember thinking that it would be pretty horrid living on it. No space to breath, to move. The man at the steering wheel didn't notice us. He just sat there, motionless, without a care in the world. He was deep in thought and smoking a pipe. I liked him.

"It was strange . . ."

"What was?"

"The pregnancy . . . The *birth*. I'd wanted him so much. I couldn't wait to hold him in my arms. I couldn't wait to touch his soft skin, to do all the things a young mother dreams of. And then it happened . . ."

"It?"

"I gave birth to him. The very moment I held him in my arms I knew I would never love him, that I would never want him . . ."

"Why? How?"

"I just knew . . . A gut feeling."

"But . . . Surely you could grow to love him?"

"Too late."

"Why?"

"He's gone . . . He doesn't belong to me."

"But don't you ever think of him?"

"Yes, but not much."

"What about now?"

"*What about now?*"

"Well, you're thinking about him now . . ."

"No, I'm not. I'm talking, not thinking. Just talking about him as I would that man on his bike over there. Or that bus on the bridge, or that beautiful tree there. He's nothing to me."

"But you gave birth to him. You carried him in your womb for nine months."

"I know I did."

"But what about . . ."

"What?"

"The father?"

"What about him?"

"Well, surely he had something to say about . . . you know . . ."

"Him? He couldn't understand much at the best of times."

"But, surely he must be angry with you? Just not caring, wanting nothing to do with your . . . with his son?"

"He didn't concern me either."

"Is he the same . . ."

". . . Man I told you about? The same man I lied about being pregnant to?"

"Yes."

"No, he's not. The father of my son is a kind man, a man full of love, a man any woman would be proud of . . . I just don't love our son, that's all."

"Are you . . ."

"Still with him?"

"Yes . . ."

"No. He left me. He took our son with him. See?"

"Yes. See what?"

"I told you he was a nice man."

We fell silent again. I was hungry. I felt hot. I felt that it might have been her causing it, but it was most probably due to the hunger—but, to be honest, I've never felt that way since. It was an odd feeling deep in my stomach. I felt light. I felt like I was floating. I wanted steak. A rare steak. With Roquefort cheese melted on it. Good thick sirloin. Only the best. I wanted to go to Elliot's Butchers on Essex Road and purchase their finest cut. Or maybe a corn-fed free-range chicken, roasted and stuffed with lemon and garlic. I would have eaten the whole thing. I began to think about roasted squash with whole, unpeeled garlic cloves and roast potatoes, roasted in goose fat. I think I began to salivate in front of her. I'm not too sure. I looked at her. She was staring straight ahead again, looking towards the snazzy flat-screen monitors. She yawned a couple of times, brushed the hair from her face, cowered slightly from the breeze. I tried to see what it was she was looking at—there were only a couple of the office workers left now. They had all gone out for lunch together or something. The man in the shirt and tie who liked to spend his working day walking back and forth from his desk to the other, over and over again, was sitting at his desk with his head in his hands. I couldn't see enough of him to gauge what colour tie he was wearing. He looked tired, troubled somewhat. But it was hard to tell. For all I knew he could have been asleep; he certainly looked like he was. He definitely had something on his mind. Maybe she was looking at him? She was certainly looking at something.

I didn't know what to do so I asked her.

"Are you hungry?"

"I don't know. I don't think so. Why?"

"Would you like to come for a coffee and a bite to eat with me? . . . I know a café just up the road from here . . . The Rheidol Café."

"No."

"Oh . . . Are you sure? You look like you . . ."

"Yes. I'm sure"

"Okay."

She didn't look up at me once. She stared steadfastly ahead towards the flat-screen monitors. I felt stupid. I tried to get up from the bench—but I couldn't. I was rooted to the spot. I felt small and quite insignificant. She suddenly turned to me.

"But, please, don't take this personally. I just don't feel like drinking coffee, or eating, or anything. That's all. I'd much rather remain here."

"Why?"

"Why what?"

"Why do you sit here?"

". . ."

"I said, why do you come to this bench each day? I told you why I did. You should tell me. It's only polite."

". . ."

"Are you not going to tell me?"

". . ."

"Are you not?"

". . ."

She remained silent. I should have gotten up from that bench there and then, maybe walked back to work— but I didn't. I simply stayed with her. It felt right. Staring straight ahead at nothing in particular. Pretty soon a swan appeared. It was probably the same one I'd noticed earlier—a magnificent creature. Beautiful in every way: so clean, so poised, stoic and aristocratic in movement. It was easily the biggest swan I had ever seen—not that I'd seen that many in my lifetime. I remember wondering why it had chosen to reside on the canal. Surely there were better places in London? Why hadn't it found itself an idyll in Kensington? Or in the suburbs? Why this grotty, uncared-for, stinking canal? It didn't make sense. Nothing made sense. She seemed not to notice the swan; she seemed in a trance, completely elsewhere. I didn't want to disturb her but I felt compelled to tell her. I couldn't help myself. I should have left her alone.

"Have you seen him?"

"Who?"

"The swan . . . There?"

"How do you know it's a he?"

"He's big. It's got to be a he."

"Well, he . . . she . . . whatever . . . is beautiful. Truly, truly beautiful."

We didn't need to say anything else. The late afternoon sun was beginning to settle. I was aware that it was probably time to go, no matter how much I wanted to stay. I wondered who came here at night. There must have been those that did? The owners of the barges lived on the other side of the canal to the right of the whitewashed office block, beyond the iron bridge. They lived private lives in a secluded enclave of lone barge owners with their own rules and etiquette. They were probably happy. I wondered if she was happy. She didn't look happy. I wondered where she went at night, whom she slept next to, whom she trusted. Did she feel safe? Did the world smother her? I wanted to know.

It seems that boredom is not really that removed from desire. It seems that they are, in fact, the same urge more or less: the urge to do something. It seems that the same common denominator underpins them: existence. And existence is essentially prolonged boredom. Desire is boredom. These urges remain with us even when the body begins to deteriorate. When the body is past its best these urges still seem to remain. They remain until the last breath. We are driven by urges we can't really explain. None of it can be explained. This, it seems to me at least, is the sheer beauty of boredom, and, more importantly, existence: It is all-powerful, more powerful than anything we can imagine.

I can't remember who got up from the bench first, but it was probably me. We didn't say goodbye to each other. I don't even think we looked at each other. We seemed to go, to move away from the bench, the canal, each other. I didn't like the idea of being on the canal at night. I had a sudden, horrible foreboding that something sinister could happen—and if it was going to happen, then it would probably happen there, when the light starts to fade, by the banks of the canal, as night began to emerge. I remember walking away, through Shepherdess Walk and up through the estate. The streets seemed to be deserted, just the orange hue of the street lamps hanging over my shoulders to guide me. I looked back—I was positive it was her, walking along behind me. It seemed odd, as she usually headed up the canal towpath towards Hackney; she never ventured into the estate. I immediately turned left onto Arlington Street and stopped. I waited for her. I could hear her footfalls as she approached. I stood out of sight, leaning against a gate to a maisonette, waiting for her to pass on the other side of the road. She didn't see me. It was definitely her. She stopped to cross the road, looking both ways. I waited until she did and then began to follow her. After a minute or so of following her I realised that she must have known I was following her. It was obvious to me that she could sense my presence. As she got to the corner of Prebend Street she was approached by a group of teenagers. I stopped. It was the same bunch from earlier that day, I'm positive; the same group that had gathered around me on the bench. Even though their hoods were up I knew it was them. It looked like they were asking her for a light. I watched as she threw up her arms, indicating to the gang that she didn't have the means to light whatever it was they wanted lighting. I hung back. I didn't want them to see me. That was the last thing I wanted. She began to walk away from them. They started laughing; one of them shouted something to her which caused the rest to fall about laughing even more. I was sure it was the lad with the red hair, but, again, it was hard to distinguish each of them from one another due to their dark clothes and hoods—due to them acting as one homogenous teenage mass. Then they turned and began to walk towards me. I turned on my heels and headed across the estate towards St Peter's Street and up towards Essex Road. It was a bit out of my way and not the route I necessarily wanted to take but I didn't want them to see me—surely things would have gotten nasty. They would've recognised me, and under the cover of the darkening streets I would have been at their mercy.

- nine -

It was raining. I momentarily considered not walking to the canal, to my bench, to her. But I did. I couldn't resist. I had been sitting on my unmade bed all morning, staring out of my window, looking at the multitudinous rooftops of Hackney. I watched the pigeons mostly, as they went about their business, only to be distracted by the civil aircraft coasting along up above them. My room sat directly underneath the flight path to Heathrow Airport. I watched the planes pass by my window, up above, in the rain. The grey cloud was a perfect backdrop. A plane seemed to pass by every two minutes or something. I counted something like fifteen Airbus A350-800s and about five or six Airbus A310s. The planes that crashed into both towers in New York were Boeing 767 200 series, wide-body, aircraft. They were big planes. I'm pretty sure none of the Airbus A350-800s were, in fact, Boeing 767s.

It was a Dan Air Boeing 727. It felt old and out of date even then. I was about seven years of age. It was a small, cramped aircraft, and I distinctly remember liking the food we were provided with. I can't remember what it was we ate. I especially liked the turbulence as we started our descent and the view from my small window. It was a night flight and everything was lit up below—even when we crossed the sea it was easy to spot the faint light from the lone ships 30,000 feet below. As a surprise my father had arranged a quick visit into the cockpit for me. I was elated. When the stewardess eventually ushered me in I was amazed to find the pilot and co-pilot casually chatting to each other like they were in the pub, or waiting at the bus stop or something. I remember thinking that I had been transported into the future. I remember thinking that everything below us, as I looked out of the cockpit's windows, was magical, transformed, beyond my ordinary imagination. When the pilot allowed me to sit in his chair, seeing the entire world below me, I remember something seeping into me that I had never felt before: importance. I felt powerful. I felt like I could control the world.

I arrived at the bench around ten a.m. The rain had abated a little. An old man was sitting on it. He was positioned dead centre and I hesitated momentarily, uncertain about which side to sit upon. I eventually opted for his left, hoping that he would shuffle up along the bench to my right. He didn't. Our legs were almost touching and I felt extremely uncomfortable. He seemed quite content with my intrusion; he was humming a tune I didn't recognise. He seemed to be humming the same part of the tune over and over again. It sounded classical; maybe Beethoven's Ninth, but I wasn't too sure. Two bags rested on the damp earth by his feet. I noticed that a soggy cigarette end was stuck to his shoe. He had a huge pot belly that hung over almost to his knees. It reminded me of my own grandfather's when he was alive. It looked rock hard, solid. His face was weathered and wrinkled like folded pasta on a plate. It didn't take me long to notice that he was missing an arm. His right arm, above the elbow. He stopped humming his tune, and, of course, it didn't take that long for him to strike up a conversation with me.

"Of course, I've travelled the world, you know. I left home at fifteen to visit China."

"Really?"

"How time has passed me by. Just another sixty years would suit me."

"Where else have you travelled to?"

"Russia. I liked Russia. Always friendly to me, the Russians. This myth that they never smile on public transport. Hogwash. Always happy to see me, the Russians."

"Really?"

"Yes. A harsh life, rough terrain, you see. Topographically unpleasant."

"Russia?"

"No, Afghanistan. Went there in my twenties, before all this stuff that's happening over there, when I was young

and as fit as a thoroughbred boxer. I wasn't no hippie. Just
curious, that's all."

"Did you travel alone?"

"Oh, yes. Always alone. Alone."

And then silence—like he had drifted off into the realm
of the dead. That was all he said. I didn't bother to continue
the conversation. I was happy with the silence.

I'm not sure what type of tree it was. I used to go there to
be alone; to do nothing, to be nothing. I was probably about
ten or eleven years of age when it started. It was my spot.
My own tree. It started much by accident: my older brother
was forced to babysit for me when my mother and father
embarked on their weekly Soho pub crawl of a Saturday
evening. One night my brother, instead of shutting himself
in his room and leaving me alone to do what I wanted,
invited about eight of his friends around to the house as
my mother and father were whisked away in the taxi. He
bundled his friends inside the house with purpose. When
they saw me there were numerous grunts, grumbles and
gesticulations towards me. They acted like I couldn't see
or hear them, like I was nothing, a blip on their landscape.
My brother shrugged his shoulders at them. Then, without
saying a word, he took me by the arm and manoeuvred me
out into the garden. He told me to wait there until he came
back. Then he walked calmly back into the house like he
owned the place. I could hear his friends laughing. He shut
the door and closed the blinds so I couldn't see inside—not
that I was in the least bit interested in them. At first I kicked
my heels and looked into next door's garden to check that
no one had seen me. Then I looked up into the night sky
for passing aircraft, but the cloud was too low and I could
only make do with the drifting ache of their engines filling

the air—one after the other behind the thick belt of cloud. I
wanted my CB radio that enabled me to tune into the pilots'
frequency so I could listen to them arrange with the control
tower their landing coordinates, but this would have meant
knocking on the back door for my brother to let me in—
which would have been impossible now that they had their
music blaring. So I walked to the tree at the bottom of the
garden and plonked myself down beneath it. The earth was
damp. I didn't care. I immediately felt safe. I immediately
felt alone. Truly alone. A strange feeling began to course
through me, to fizz in my bones: a nothingness, an emptiness: Boredom. It glued me to the spot. The whole world
could have imploded and I wouldn't have cared. I was de-
liriously happy.

I must have dozed off because when I looked back up to my
right the old man with one arm had gone and she was there
sitting beside me. She looked different. It took me a while to
notice that her clothes weren't as colour coordinated as usual—for all I know this could have always been the case—in
fact there seemed to be no coordination whatsoever. She was
wearing red Converse All-Stars and tight black jeans; her v-
neck sweater looked about two sizes to big for her; her hair
was ruffled and she carried what looked like a Burberry's
Mack under her arm—navy blue—but it could have been
Aquascutum. It was quite an incongruous look for her. It
was the first time I noticed that she was probably younger
than me—maybe eight or nine years younger. It was hard
to tell. She began to yawn, as per usual. I had never known
anyone to yawn as much as her, far too long for comfort,
long drawn-out things that seemed to last perfect aeons. She
did this like it was the most natural thing in the world and
I was sure that she would break into such antics no matter
where she was or whom she was with: a first date, a job

interview, during sex, at a friend's funeral. She began to rub the palm of her left hand with her right thumb, slowly at first, but then with more vim and determination. She seemed to be thinking about something. Something seemed to be troubling her.

"Hullo."

"Hullo."

"I didn't see you arrive . . ."

"That's because you were asleep . . . *Snoring* . . . I've been here for a while actually."

"Oh . . . How embarrassing . . . What have you been doing?"

"Nothing."

"You look tired . . . Date last night?"

"No."

"Did you go out?"

"No."

"Friends?"

"No."

"What did you do then?"

"Nothing. I told you. Nothing."

"Nothing, *really*?"

"Nothing."

"Oh."

". . ."

". . ."

"I like to watch the planes . . ."

"I like to paint . . ."

"You do?"

"Yes, I do . . ."

"What's your name?"

"Oh, come on! How many times are you going to ask me this? You don't need to know my name, like I don't yours. Let's leave it at that, okay?"

"Hmmmm."

"Okay?"

"Well, okay, what do you paint?"

"Not much."

"When do you find the time to paint? You're always here."

"I just paint when I can; I don't much like it. I paint with my own blood—I mix it in with the paint. Always acrylic. Mostly faces, faces of me. No one really knows their own face, not even when looking into a mirror. As I do when trying to memorise mine . . . We can never be truly objective."

"But they're still self portraits?"

"Maybe."

"Why do you paint in your own blood? Does that . . . Is that painful for you?"

"I don't know . . . It's not that it has a better texture or anything . . . It's just the same as if I painted without. Why not paint in my own blood? Most people who paint just mix in water. What is the point in that? Not putting in anything of yourself, I mean?"

"There's no point, I guess. I don't know much about painting. I never took to it. Art, modern art, galleries, artists, they leave me cold . . ."

"I want all my paintings to be destroyed. I like a good cull. I destroy most of them myself. They hold no meaning for me, how could they?"

"What do you mean?"

"I paint for myself and no one else. I paint because I will one day die. Because I want to die. Because I hate myself. Each time I destroy one of my paintings I am destroying part of myself. I am a cliché and I like it that way . . ."

"I don't understand."

"There's nothing to understand. *Nothing.*"

"What do you mean?"

"It's all meaningless."

"What is?"

"This is."

"Us?"

"No."

"What, then?"

"This . . . This . . . This is a mask. I wear it. I say I paint to people so they can have a mental image of me . . ."

"So you don't paint?"

"Yes, I do paint . . . It's my mask."

"Mask?"

"People wear masks. They are forced upon them. These masks, they do not even know they are wearing them. These masks help them to exist, to co-habit within society. They are clowns for it . . . I am aware of my mask, as clichéd as it seems. As clichéd as it *is*. It's why I want to end my life, why I find life, society, so obvious, *so ugly*. And those who don't, those clowns, find life so entertaining."

Again, she began to yawn. I looked over to the white-washed offices; the man who spent his working hours walking from desk to desk was standing motionless by a photocopying machine. He was wearing a white shirt, a red tie, and a grey cardigan that looked a size too small for him. The murky water of the canal was bereft of life: not a swan, goose, or coot in sight. Even the banks were empty of pigeons. The murky water was calm, the slight swirl of a thin layer of scum and oil broke the stillness, its thick stench heavy in the damp air.

Each Saturday morning I used to accompany my mother on a bus ride to the other side of London to visit my grand-mother—on my father's side—for the day. She never took the tube because she thought it a breeding ground for germs and pestilence. I took this journey with my mother every Saturday up until the age of twelve, when my mother finally learnt how to drive. I may have been six years of age on this occasion. I was sitting at the bus stop with my mother. The bus, as usual, was late. Behind the bus stop was a public house called The Willow Tavern, which has long since been demolished and flats with large balconies have been built on its land. In front of the pub there used to be a car park. The car park was surrounded by a chain-link fence, fitted with thick spikes on each link. I presumed this was to deter people from driving straight from the road, over the pavement, and onto the car park when the pub was closed. Pubs don't seem to have these same spiked, linked fences any longer, at least I haven't seen any. I remember being bored and walking over and sitting on it, between two spikes. It started to sway like a swing in a playground and I began to purposely push myself forward and backwards, forward and backwards with relative ease. And then, before I could figure out what was happening, there was sudden blackness. Just blackness. Warm, like a large duvet had been pulled over me. When I opened my eyes my mother was crouched down over me. She was crying, a frantic look upon her face. Two strangers—an old man and woman whose faces have never left me—were also standing over me.

"He's opened his eyes."

"He's opened them."

"*Oh, son . . . Son . . . Son . . .*"

"He's okay, lady."

"He's shaken . . ."

"Oh, son . . ."

I quite enjoyed the trip in the ambulance at first. I remember the sirens in particular; I was quite content for a moment. And then I noticed the blood. Blood, *my blood*, was everywhere. I was covered in it, my mother was covered in it—the paramedics' hands were covered in it. I reached a hand around to the back of my head. Fear gripped me instantly. I remember thinking that I was going to die. I remember—like it was only yesterday—being convinced that I was dying, that there was nothing anyone—my mother, the paramedics—could do for me. I remember starting to shake, to holler and scream. I became convinced the ambulance was taking me to the hospital to die. My memories of this unpleasant episode are bathed in red. Blood red. The sickly sight of my own blood. I began to wail.

"Is it my blood? Is it my blood? Is it my blood? Is it my blood? Is it my blood? Is it my blood? Is it my blood? Is it my blood? Is it my blood? Is it my blood? Is it my blood? Is it my blood? Is it my blood? Is it my blood? Is it my blood? Is it my blood?"

My mother, still sobbing, held me and told me that everything was going to be okay, that I would be fine. For the first time in my life I didn't believe her. I was convinced otherwise. I continued to think that I was dying. I continued to ask her over and over again all the way to the hospital, I remember it like it was yesterday.

"Am I going to die, mum? Am I going to die, mum? Am I going to die, mum? Am I going to die, mum? Am I going to die, mum? Am I going to die, mum? Am I going to die, mum? Am I going to die, mum? Am I going to die, mum? Am I going to die, mum? Am I going to die, mum? Am I going to die, mum? Am I going to die, mum? Am I going to die, mum? Am I going to die, mum? Am I going to die, mum? Am I going to die, mum?"

I was convinced. My mother soothed my head, shushing me all the while.

"Shush . . . Shush . . . Shush . . ."

*   *   *

The clouds suddenly began to darken like a giant bruise across the sky and a breeze picked up around our ears. My right leg began to shake. I was anxious. I wanted to pick her up and take her with me somewhere. To the Rheidol Café. Anywhere. I wanted to be with her and the longer these silences persisted the stronger grew my urge. Little by little she was beginning to consume me. But I didn't know what to say. I didn't know what to do. I kept on looking at her, waiting for something, waiting for her to do something. She was still looking over at the whitewashed office block. I'm sure she was looking directly at the man with the white shirt, red tie, and grey cardigan one size too small. I'm positive she was.

I don't think I've ever been in love with anyone—I seriously think I'm incapable of love in that way: to actually *love* someone. I have certainly felt love for things, I have felt the love of others, but I seriously don't think I have ever loved anyone. The closest thing I ever felt to feeling love for someone was a long time ago now. It was a girl, we fleetingly lived with each other. We used to spend all day in bed together, only getting out from the bed to either piss or prepare food. One Sunday she spent the whole day colouring in each individual freckle on my right leg with a blue Biro. Each freckle as unique as a snowflake. She spent all day doing this, tattooing each individual freckle, each individual shape with her blue Biro. It literally took all day. I lay there, allowing her to do this, quite curious, as she worked on each individual freckle patiently, with tenderness and care. The light outside was beginning to fade when she finally finished her task—although we could never be certain she had actually coloured in each and every freckle. When I finally looked in the mirror, at first glance it looked like my entire leg was blue, but on closer inspection I could locate each individual freckle. I didn't know I had so many.

I hadn't realised. I'd never given it much thought before. I had more freckles than unblemished skin it seemed. I liked that. I kissed her passionately. Then I became concerned that I might get ink poisoning. It took me a full hour in a hot shower to scrub each individual dab of delicate blue Biro off. I felt like we had achieved something, that we had both discovered something together.

But it wasn't love. I've never felt it. This was never a problem until I started visiting that bench each day. I often think of people in love, those who have spent their entire lives together, as deeply bored—they must be, to want to spend a whole life together. Nothing must force them to part, to walk away, to do something different. Their boredom must be channelled into this thing they believe in, this word: love. They must never think about it: the boredom, as it pours into them, convincing them that their love means something. That there is deep meaning in all the years they spend together. I don't know about that. I think those types of people are scared: scared of being alone, scared of emptiness, scared of dying alone: scared of boredom.

Although, I soon began to think about love too. I began to think about love quite a lot—as much as I think about boredom, in fact.

And then they walked over to us. They seemed to appear from out of nowhere, from within the murky ether of the canal. That same gang, those same four teenagers who accosted me the day I was alone. The lad with the red hair I didn't trust. They were dressed in exactly the same clothes. The red-haired one looked dirtier though, unkempt, like he'd been sleeping rough. They seemed to know her—or at least recognised her from the other day, when they asked her for a light in the street—pointing at her in unison as they approached.

"Hey, it's you, man."

"You're here again, man."

"With that battyboy, man"

"You and him, man."

She didn't seem too fussed by their immediate and abrupt presence. In fact, she seemed to let it wash over her, even when they began to sit next to her, cutting me out, leaning in close to her and flicking her hair from time to time.

"JC reckons he could have you, girl."

"He want you, girl, so much."

"He could have you like that, girl."

"Yeah, I want you, girl, I want you."

She seemed to brush off their crude advances like one would a fly from one's food in mid-conversation: nonchalantly and without a care in the world, second nature. It was the one with the red hair who started to touch her leg. She shivered. But she didn't once try to move away. I looked across. I looked at his grimy hand on her leg, above the knee. He was squeezing it. His three friends giggling like the children they actually were—she just sat there. I had to say something, even if that something would pique their attention enough to turn violent with me. I had to say something.

"Take your fucking hand off her leg!"

It came out like that. I said it loudly. I almost shouted it. The four teenagers looked at me.

"What did you just say, man?"

"What did you say, man?"

"What's that, man?"

"You talking our way, man?"

They began to surround me. She turned to me; I looked at her. She shook her head, instructing me not to say any more, but I couldn't help myself.

"Don't fucking touch her again . . . ."

My right leg was shaking. The first one to hit me was the tallest one, the one with the shaved head: the blow came full in the side of my head. It hurt. The force of it pushing me from the bench and onto the ground. Then they began kicking me and I could feel nothing, except each thud as their feet dug into my ribs and bounced off my head. It felt as if the air had been sucked out of my lungs. I couldn't breathe. I couldn't hear anything. Then the shock of blackness.

Then nothing.

When I awoke they had gone. So had she. I crawled back to the bench. I looked over to the whitewashed office block: everyone was staring over at me: groups gathered at each looming window. Why hadn't they tried to do something? Why hadn't they shouted over, or called the police? My face began to throb. My ribs felt like they had been plucked from me. I found it difficult to breathe but I guessed that I was okay. My pockets were empty and my wallet had been taken. I knew I didn't want to get the police involved; I knew I didn't want to get anyone involved. But I wanted to know where she had gone to. It baffled me. I started to walk. Back towards Hackney. I needed to get to a phone box to inform my bank to cancel my cash card. I needed to walk towards where I thought she might be. I figured she might live in the De Beauvoir Town area, or somewhere in that location. It suited her. She looked that type: one of those individuals content to sit in a gastro-pub playing scrabble or backgammon with the one they love.

Just as I was about to leave the canal towpath I noticed the swan on the murky water. It was looking directly at me. Right at me. Into me. Like it knew something I didn't. I stopped walking. It came up to me. It knew I had no food for it, but still it came, right up to the edge of the towpath. I knelt down slowly, painfully, and stretched out my hand to stroke its head, thinking to myself that it would shy away off in the opposite direction from me, but it didn't; the swan allowed me to stroke its head and long neck, like it was a domesticated cat or something. This huge swan before me, allowing me to stroke it. It was the most incredible thing. Never had I seen such a thing before, and I certainly hadn't had such a thing happen to me before. The huge, white swan and me. Friends.

The swan came to me. It came to me.

PART TWO

- conversation one -

"Why do you always tell me these . . ."
    "*Secrets*?"
    "Yes, these secrets?"
    "Because it's easy."
    "Why don't you tell me anything else?"
    "As I said, there's nothing else to say."
    "But . . ."
    "But what?"
    "But there's lots to say."
    "It's all been said before. Plus, the silences are just as important."
    "*Silences*?"
    "Those times we don't say anything . . . It's when we say the most."
    "I don't understand . . ."
    "You don't have to . . ."
    "But I want you to tell me things."
    "*Things*?"
    "Things about you . . ."
    "I have done . . ."
    "Not enough."

"Never enough."

The sun was shining. The bruises on my face were beginning to fade. Thankfully, I hadn't seen the gang of teenagers in the few days that had passed since they had attacked me. Before walking back to the bench I had spent most of my time in bed, watching downloads on my laptop, and thinking of her, and when my bones eventually stopped aching, and my flesh had begun to heal, I plucked up the courage to walk back to her. I hadn't mentioned the attack to anyone. There was no need to talk it through with her—our meetings weren't about me. At least that's how it seemed. Sitting on the bench had been a pleasant experience; the previous days in bed had been bliss, albeit a little painful.

It was on this day, and for the first time, that I noticed she had not one, as I had earlier thought, but two small, inoffensive moles on her right cheek. One seemed slightly bigger than the other. I didn't think that she had been hiding these from me; I supposed I simply hadn't noticed them together. I was noticing new things about her all the time. For instance: her mouth twitched when she was thinking or daydreaming, before she was about to say something—or say nothing. She would sometimes break off mid-sentence, abruptly stop for no apparent reason, but such were her words and intentions that not once did this cause me any confusion. She always seemed to have new cuts and bruises on her elbows and knees, little abrasions, bruises and marks. Little things about her began to pour into me—little by little I was beginning to see who she really was. At least that's how it felt. And the less she said the more I understood. That's how it was. And her *lessness* made it all the more terrifying.

Her skin was beautiful, a most wonderful colour, like freshly sanded-down wood. It revealed itself almost mockingly. I was embarrassed that I hadn't noticed these things

about her before; it infuriated me somewhat. She had told
me things I had never heard anyone speak of. At first, I
thought she must have been lying for some reason, that she
must have been taking me for a fool. But she wasn't. She
was telling the truth, and there was no point in me trying to
fathom how I knew that it was, and that was all I needed
to know. This had all happened to me the previous couple
of days, I think. Just after my bed-rest, when I was still sore
with aches and sharp, stabbing pains, when I looked at her
differently. I don't think I'll ever be able to forget what she
told me.

"In order for us to continue meeting like this there are
two fundamental things you should know about me."

This is what she said to me, how it all started, how I
remember it, on the bench, the commuters passing us by.

It was around midday.

"What do you mean?"

"I've always liked cars."

"Okay."

"Ever since I was a young girl I always wanted to own
one. My peers all had dreams of fairy-tale weddings, money,
big houses, clothes, and boyfriends, husbands and children.
I just wanted a car. On my seventeenth birthday I took my
first lesson. I was a natural . . . It was easy. I passed the
test my first time without breaking a sweat. At first, I used
to use my father's Volvo up until I bought my own. My
first car . . . I saved up all year . . . A bashed-up old VW
Beetle. It was an original, not one of the new things. It was
blue. It never got me anywhere. Always breaking down on
me . . ."

"Ha! I like them! Those old Beetles . . ."

"I loved it. I had a name for it, too . . . If you want to
know then don't bother asking, I won't tell you. We went
everywhere together. Even if I had to go to the shops or

make a phone call, I would drive up to the top of the street and use the phone box, my bashed-up old blue Beetle parked outside where I could see it. It's funny, I could have walked there and back in the time it took me to grab my keys, my shoes, drive around the block and find a parking space. But I didn't care. Like I said, I never went anywhere without my car. It was the saddest day of my life when she was written off. The day she was hit face on. She was stationary, parked there, where I always parked her of an evening, when the other car hit her. I still have bits of her, though, like the steering wheel, the gear stick . . . That's it."

"That's a shame . . ."

"It happens."

"It's still a shame . . ."

There was pause in our conversation. The whole canal was extraordinarily quiet. I watched her pull her brown skirt down to cover her slightly bruised knees. Her mouth twitched to the right and then to the left, and then back to the right again. Then she looked at me. It was a vacant stare. It was without any trace of emotion, like there was nothing inside her, as if she was beautifully hollow. And then she continued.

"Something happened to me last year."

"Oh."

"Yes."

"What do you mean?"

"I was in a car."

"A crash?"

"Something like that, I suppose . . ."

"What happened?"

"It's difficult for me to say. I've never mentioned this to anyone before. I don't even know why I'm about to tell you, I shouldn't be mentioning this to anyone—it should be extinguished from my mind, but I can't, I can't put it out of my mind. I don't think I can until I have told someone . . . *you* . . . do you understand?"

"I think so . . ."

"I hit someone . . ."

"You *hit* someone?"

"Yes."

"Yeah?"

"In my car . . ."

"In *your* car?"

"Yes, while I was driving in my car . . . I hit someone."

"You mean you knocked someone over?"

"Well . . . yes . . . I suppose so. In my car . . . my perfect machine."

"Was it an accident?"

". . ."

"Was it an accident? Did you . . . ?"

". . ."

"What happened? Tell me."

"I meant to hit him . . . I had every intention of hitting him . . . I headed straight for him . . . I *wanted* to hit him . . . To *hit* him."

"Where?"

"What do you mean *where*?"

"Where did this happen?"

"Before I tell you *when* and *where* this happened please allow me to tell you about my car, the car I was driving . . ."

"I don't know anything about cars . . ."

"You don't need to. You just need to know what type of car it is . . ."

"But even if you told me I wouldn't be able to visualise it, I just don't know enough about these things . . . *cars* . . . that sort of stuff."

"Then I will explain in as much detail as I can so that you can at least visualise something . . . The car, my car, is integral, you see."

"Oh . . . Okay, I understand."

"The car I was driving, on the night I hit him, was an Audi TT 225 . . ."

I don't know why I was so interested in what she was saying to me as until that moment I'd never thought about learning to drive a car, let alone owning one, and people who often talked about cars—groups of lads in pubs and at work, et cetera—sickened me to such an extent that I had to get up and remove myself from the conversation. But this was different. I have often asked myself what I would use a car for—if I could, in fact, drive. Certainly not for long drives in the country, or to visit relatives on the other side of London; such things weren't for me. I like the distance as it is. I'm not averse to people giving me lifts to places if I am in a rush or stuck or something. I don't mind that. But that's as far as it goes. I'd have to have had a really good reason to have bought my own car.

I've been involved in one car crash in my lifetime. I was seventeen years of age. I know this for certain as it was on my birthday. My parents had offered to pay for driving lessons but I told them that I didn't want them. Three of us were in the car that crashed: me, Mike McCooty, and some lad whose name I have since forgotten. We were somewhere in Epping on a long, winding lane. Mike McCooty was driving, I was in the passenger seat and the other lad was in the back, laying across the back seat, his feet resting outside the open window of the right-hand door, like he was in a hammock. I can still recall the tyres screeching as we tore through each bend. It happened quite quickly, the crash:

another car came hurtling around a blind corner which caused us to swerve and brake abruptly, skidding up the embankment to our immediate left. The car—it was silver, that's all I can recall—flipped, the engine revving uncontrollably as we lay in a crumpled heap on the underside of the roof. None of us were wearing our seatbelts and it was lucky we weren't injured. All I remember is Mike McCooty laughing hysterically as the lad in the back lay screaming like a baby. It was me who first noticed the thick acrid smoke pluming from the engine. I remember feeling a peculiar excitement: that's all it took, snap, crack, bang, like that—anything could take you away. It could happen at any time. I remember thinking that this didn't bother me. We climbed out of the open window in the back of the car and stood by the embankment, looking at the crumpled wreck before us, until the police arrived. The driver of the other car—an elderly lady—was just pleased that no one was hurt or wanted to accuse her of reckless driving.

The last I'd heard of Mike McCooty he'd made millions importing discontinued Adidas trainers to feed the consuming habits of the burgeoning Indie and Retro markets. The other lad: I have no idea; he could be dead for all I know.

"I, er, know nothing about them, sorry . . . about cars in general . . ."

"It doesn't matter that you don't know. Really, it doesn't. What matters is that this was it . . ."

"*It?*"

"The real deal . . . *The car* . . . The car of my dreams . . . The car I'd been waiting for all my life. I owned nothing else in comparison . . ."

"Tell me about it then."

"The car? Or what happened?"

"The car . . . and then what happened."

"It's an Audi TT 225 Quattro Coupe. It's a powerful little machine able to explode from zero to sixty in six point six seconds flat. A top speed of one hundred and fifty-one miles per hour. Although, I'm positive I've pushed it further. It's specified in pearl-effect black with a grey leather interior. But the wheels—perfect seven and a half by seventeen inch rims. People would turn heads whenever I sped by. It's really my ultimate machine. You should see the engine—seventeen eighty-one cc's in size, gleaming all year round."

"Your pride and joy?"

"More than that."

"I don't understand . . ."

"It's simple: we are technology—we rival nature. We are able to mould ourselves into something superior. Put simply, my car means more to me than any other thing I can think of . . ."

"But you sit here every day . . ."

"I haven't set foot behind a wheel since it happened . . ."

"Since what happened?"

"The day I hit that man . . ."

"Was it . . . ?"

"What?"

"Was it a . . . ?"

"Hit and run?"

"Yes."

"Yes . . . it was."

"Did he . . . ?"

"What?"

"Did you . . . ?"

"Kill him?"

"Yes . . ."

". . ."

"Did you kill him?"

". . ."

"Did you?"

"Yes, I *killed* him."

I sank into the bench. I could feel each grain, each fibre of it beneath me. She seemed to perk up; her back straightened, her posture a textbook example.

"I got out of the car and looked at him. He was dead. Crumpled. Bleeding. His eyes were open. He was facing me, his blood-red face. It was like he was looking at me, right at me, but I knew he wasn't . . . I knew he was dead. And he was smiling. He was smiling. I swear he was smiling. And I knew no one else could see us. And I knew I could just drive away without being seen. I knelt down beside him, I could smell him. I can remember that smell right now . . . Beer, cigarettes . . . *pubs* . . . I wanted to kiss his wet lips, crinkled and split as they were. For weeks after I hit him, after the news reporters and newspapers had long forgotten about him, I polished my car over and over. I had it repaired under a railway arch in Hackney, near London Fields. Cash in hand, no questions asked. I polished my car. I polished it until no trace of that night could be detected. I became obsessed with making it shine. I awaited sunny days. I wanted light to shine from it. That night, after I hit him, I took a kitchen knife, a small vegetable knife for paring, and cut my arm . . . a small incision. I let the blood drip down to my fingertips, I let it drip until I felt numb . . . until I fell asleep."

She turned to me. She inched closer to me. We were almost touching. I noticed something in her eyes that I hadn't noticed before: there was life in them; they were fizzing, intense, real. She looked excited. She looked alive. Her eyes weren't the dark pools of emptiness and sorrow I was led to believe they were. I could see past all that. If she would have cried at that moment her tears wouldn't have been silent, they would have been noisy, vibrant tears— tears that mocked anyone who tried to wipe them away. I wanted to touch her face, her smooth skin, her cheek. This incredible urge raged within me. I wanted to kiss her. When she continued with her confession, it felt like I was melting into the bench. It felt like nothing else mattered, like nothing around us actually existed. And then it dawned on me as she continued: her eyes were elsewhere.

"I would polish my TT most days, every day sometimes. I couldn't stand the London grime, the pollution. I would wipe it away constantly. My car had to be pristine at all times. I wasn't affected, there was nothing wrong with me. There was, and is, no meaning in my constant attention to cleanliness. I just wanted my TT, *my car*, to be clean. If I saw other TTs on the road that looked newer, cleaner, I would turn back, or pull up at the nearest car wash. Mine had to be cleaner, the cleanest . . ."

"But it was only a car . . ."

"It was . . . *is* . . . my car . . . *my car* . . ."

"I don't understand . . ."

"You don't have to. It's all very simple. We were fused: my self . . . my car . . . fused. Atomised. I would polish my TT until I could see every wrinkle in my face when I peered into its finish. I had boyfriends who would become jealous of the time and attention I dedicated to it. They would complain to me. It wasn't their fault, they could have never have understood."

"Okay, okay . . . So, if you loved the car so much, then why did you end it all by . . ."

"By running into him?"

"Yes."

"Because I could."

"You must have had a reason."

"No. No reason. Just impulse."
"Impulse?"
"Yes."

I've always been able to understand impulse. It is something
that is instantly recognisable to me. It is something that is
tangible, that I have felt, intrinsically, throughout my life.
Even as a young child I understood impulse. I understood
that there were no real reasons to my actions, as much as
anyone else's. I wouldn't necessarily call myself a violent
man, but, on impulse, I have acted violently. Such violent
impulses have happened only twice in my life, and both
incidences involved me hitting other people. The first time
it happened I was a small child, I can hardly remember it.
All I know is that it happened in a park, by a sand pit: I hit
another child playing in the sand pit. The second time was
a number of years ago. It involved my then closest friend.
I will not mention his name here. We had been drinking
happily all day and were walking home to the flat we then
shared together in Hackney, near the elevated railway lines.
We weren't even arguing, and nothing had rankled within
me. I just had the sudden impulse to hit him—maybe it was
something he said, I don't know. I hit him on the side of
the head with my fist, a drunken right hook, executed with
little, if any, technique that somehow landed with force and
knocked him off balance. He fell sideways, landing awkwardly on his arm by the curb. His arm snapped like a twig.
I am positive I heard the snap. He was in incredible pain.
I don't think I felt guilty at the time. I calmly escorted him
to A&E. We sat next to each other in silence. People were
shouting at nurses, teenagers were puking into buckets,
drunks were lighting up cigarettes. Overworked doctors ran
amok. He moved out of the flat shortly afterwards, and we
have never spoken to or seen each other since. I often think

of that night now; it haunts me when I am alone; it visits my dreams. The clear sound of his ulna snapping: it visits me when I walk down the street, or at home washing the dishes. I cannot escape it. It is obvious to me now that most acts of violence are caused by those who are truly bored. And as our world becomes increasingly boring, as the future progresses into a quagmire of nothingness, our world will become increasingly more violent. It is an impulse that controls us. It is an impulse we cannot ignore.

"But I don't want to talk about impulse just yet . . ."

"No?"

"No . . . I want to talk about Jonathan Richman . . ."

"Who?"

"He is a musician . . . *The Modern Lovers* . . . He wrote what is considered to be the first ever modern punk record . . ."

"Oh, what was it called?"

"*Roadrunner*. It's probably my favourite song of all time. Do you have a favourite song?"

"Not really . . ."

"I was . . ."

"What?"

"I was listening to it when . . ."

"When what?"

"When I hit him . . ."

"But why are you telling me all this? Why? Why me? What's the point in telling me all this in such detail? What's the point?"

" . . ."

"Well? Why? What's the point in telling me all this?

" . . ."

" . . ."

"Music is important . . . It is integral to our understanding of things."

"*Things?*"

"Yes. Things. Stuff. *Everything.*"

"Oh."

"That song . . . *Roadrunner* . . . has stuck with me for
a long time. I just knew that it would be around on such an
important day."

"Why?"

"It had to be . . ."

"But, I don't understand . . ."

"I've told you before, you don't have to *understand*.
There's nothing *to* understand . . ."

"We're going around in circles . . ."

"That's not a concern of mine. But just to listen to
that song as you're hurtling down an open road. Such an
amazing feeling . . . Really. It's originally about route 128
in Boston, a circular like the M25, although, it's not exactly
circular. Travelling north or south is just the same as travelling round and round in circles anyway, isn't it? Anyway,
it is Richman's car journey I'm interested in, the journey
he undertakes throughout each version of the song . . . *the
same song* . . . There are many versions of it."

"There's more than one version?"

"There are many versions. All are a homage to the turn-
pike, the industrial park, the North Shore, the South Shore,
the Prudential Tower, the Sheraton Tower, the everyday
nothingness of the peripheries of Boston, noting each as
he passes them by over and over and over again. I've read
about the excitement he used to feel speeding over the hill,
catching sight for the first time that day of the radio towers in the distance. He'd see beauty in these humdrum
things . . . I used to drive listening to him, I used to look

for the same things, the same type of beauty he did . . . It was everywhere I looked . . . I see that, too, *I do*, that same beauty in things . . . the ordinary things."

"I know you do . . ."

It seemed as if we were melting into each other, her scent enveloping me, soaking into me like never before. I wanted to say so much to her; I wanted to do so many things with her; with no one else. I wanted nothing else to exist, so we could get up and walk somewhere together: a pub, a café, a park, even a gallery. Anywhere. I wanted to do something.

But I couldn't.

I was truly spellbound.

I started to think about those teenagers who attacked me, the Pack Crew. I wondered what they might have been doing at that precise moment. My body was aching all over because of them. They had acted on that same impulse. They had chosen to harm me, to hurt me for no other reason: boredom. They were bored. They always would be. They are never ending.

I wondered to myself what they would do with themselves if only they knew what I did: I hoped it would be nothing. Absolutely nothing.

"You're thinking about why I hit him, aren't you?"

"No . . . I'm thinking about something else . . . Those . . ."

"I hit him because I knew it would feel good . . . I was hypnotised . . . I truly was. I knew what I had to do . . . I just knew."

"How can it *feel good*? How can something like that *feel good*?"

"You can't imagine how good it feels. To wipe something out. To wipe something out completely."

"Why's that?"

"Because you've never done it."

"Where did it happen?"

"In the outskirts of the city, Blackheath way, on a lonely road . . . the light pollution from the city filling the night sky in the distance. It looked like it had been painted on by some amateur."

"What did?"

"The light in the sky in the distance. It looked faked, *inauthentic* . . . I loved it because it was still real."

"Do you know anything about him?"

"The man?"

"Yes, the *man*."

"I know lots. Before I hit him I knew nothing. Now I know everything. It was in the papers, on the local news. I found out all I needed to know about him."

"Why did you do that?"

"Because I *had* to . . . I've never been caught. No one knows it was me. I have escaped my punishment . . . for the time being, anyhow. I needed to find out about him in order to understand his life . . . He was a pointless man, a meaningless human being. One of many. A security guard at a bank in the city. He'd worked there for twenty years. He was divorced, a small family. He was close to his son and a couple of lifelong friends he used to drink with. He was a season ticket holder at Charlton FC. That's it."

"What was his name?"

"Haven't you listened to a *word* I've said to you?"

"Yes, that's why I ask."

"T____ E_____"

"Don't you feel any guilt?"

"No."

"Why?"

"I don't know . . . Maybe I'm scared?"

"Just tell me why you did it."

"I had to do it. I saw him and . . . I had to obliterate him from my life. I had to make him obsolete. There was no other option . . . It felt good, butterflies in my stomach, that type of thing, some call it a *buzz* . . . My god, the sound of the engine as I approached him, dropping a gear, there was nothing I could do except hit him."

"Stop!"

"Why?"

"It's just too awful. You killed a man!"

"*He was already dead before I hit him.*"

"What does that mean?"

"He didn't matter. *We* don't matter. If you could have felt what I felt behind that wheel—just the rumble, the slight tremor of surface movement, of things, bitumen, passing beneath me. The speed . . . the engine growling . . . We are limited. We need something more, we need that added extra in life. Technology provides all we need. Technology dominates a large part of our unique relationship with the exterior world. I have never wanted to hide behind technology. I have always wanted to use it, to control it, to display it. It has always puzzled me why one would want to hide one's hearing aid away from the world. Why do that? Do you understand? It is an extension. That's all. Part of us . . . All of us should understand that technology will be the death of us, not our saviour . . . It's leaving us all behind. I am just repeating the obvious."

"Just please explain to me what happened on the night you hit him?"

"I *am*. I had an argument . . ."

"With him?"

"No, with the man I was seeing at that time. A good man, a man who knew nothing other than working hard for a living, providing for those he loved. A man who bought what he was told to buy. A man who simply lived. A good man. We argued . . . We hated each other, we wanted no part in each other. So I got in my car. I got away from him . . . I've never seen him since. I think."

, "Why?"

"Because I've never wanted to, that's why."

"You said *I think* . . ."

". . ."

"So you have seen him since?"

". . ."

"I thought so."

"But I'm not lying to you. This is the truth. I've never told anyone this before. I was driving . . . *away* . . . I just wanted to get away from him. I was taken by the views of the city. I could see everything there was to see. It was all sprawled out before me. I was alive. I felt connected to the night. My TT. Me, alone, away from him . . . And then I saw him, he was just standing there. I saw him. I passed him. He didn't see me, so I followed the road. I knew it would take me back around. I knew it would take me back to him. I had been driving for about two hours, just around and around the M25. I sometimes liked to do that—eighty-ninety miles per hour and heading absolutely nowhere, just around and around, just driving along. I got off somewhere near Dartford. I found myself on Shooters Hill Road heading towards Blackheath. I circled the heath a few times, not really knowing where to go. The streets were completely deserted just off the main drag. I remember thinking it looked odd. I felt strange. It was maybe three a.m., but the reports in the media stated that he was hit sometime between one-thirty and two-thirty a.m. I saw him walking towards Wemyss Road from Paragon Place. He was walking slowly and looked like he had been drinking. The news reports said that he had been drinking with his work colleagues. Apparently he was far away from home and was probably trying to flag down a taxi. But he looked local to me. He looked like he belonged. Apparently he socialised with work colleagues each Thursday night . . . I followed along Paragon Place. He must have sensed me, as he started to quicken his pace. He didn't look at me, not once . . . Not that time, anyway. I slowed alongside him, but he just stared at his feet. I crawled alongside him for about ten metres before I continued down Paragon Place and onto Wemyss Road. I immediately turned left onto Montpelier Row, continuing onto Prince of Wales Road. It was there that I decided to go back around to Paragon Place again, to see if he was still there, dawdling along. He had ventured onto Wemyss Road. I pulled up behind him and turned off all my lights . . . Just my stereo playing, that song, *that perfect song* . . . I think I hit him at about forty miles per hour just as he stepped into the road to cross to the other side. It was perfect timing, as if it had been rehearsed many times. It was like he'd been suddenly plucked up from the ground and flung mercilessly into the night. He hit the curb head first behind me and probably died on impact. I looked at his crumpled body through my rearview mirror. My heart was beating quickly, so quickly, so frantically. I backed up the TT to get a closer look. I got out. His eyes were wide open, just staring up into the night. And that smile on his face, I'll never forget that smile. The one thing I regret—the one thing that haunts me—is that I should never have gotten out of the TT. I should have remained inside. I should've remained intact . . . I wasn't too bothered about the damage at the front of my car. Like I said, I knew of places where I could get that fixed . . . He was nothing to me, just some random human being. I just had to do it . . . because I could. If they find me—which *they* at some point will—I still won't be able to answer their questions. I'll never be able to answer them. Not the absolute. All I can say, all that I could tell them, the one thing . . . his eyes . . . as I approached him, just as he stepped out onto the road, he turned and looked directly at me. At least this is how I remember it now. He looked at me . . . *into me*, you know? Just before I hit him. *Just before I hit him.*"

"I don't know what to say . . ."

"You don't have to say anything. I just had to tell you this . . . It's funny."

"What is?"

"I almost wish that I could go back . . . just to see . . ."

"What for?"

"To see if he was really looking at me . . ."

I once looked up on the internet the most common injuries relating to hit-and-run incidents. There weren't that many I could think of without help. The injuries were countless: traumatic brain injury, skull fractures and haematoma, along with extensive damage to hands, arms, forearms, shoulders, and wrists. Fingers are often crushed. Lower limb damage to legs, hips, knees, heels, and feet are also extremely common. Hidden internal injuries are manifold: torn spleens and severe damage to organs, such as the heart, kidneys, liver, bowels, lungs, and the aorta often lead to internal bleeding. The whole spectacle is a bloody, rotten mess. I have never stopped to look at car accidents for this very reason.

The canal was silent. Not a sound could be heard. It was as if the wind had taken it all away. I looked to my feet. I didn't know what to do, what to say. I imagined it happening all over London, the entire country: gleaming cars hitting tired, worn-out random people, in random streets, in random towns, and random cities. I imagined it occurring all over the world: the cool exterior of each car smashing into warm living flesh.

"Do you fancy coming to get something to eat with me . . . ?"

"I'm not hungry. Telling you all this has left me feeling cold. I'm going to leave now."

"Oh. Okay."

"Will you be here tomorrow?"

"Yes . . . I will."

"Good. So will I . . ."

- conversation two -

"Where were you on Thursday, the seventh of July, 2005?"

"The bombings?"

"Yes."

"I was walking to work. The same job I have just left . . . recently . . . I was on Moorgate wondering why the streets were swamped, people walking in the road, police on every corner, and why the majority of people were walking towards me, away from Bank, away from the square mile, the City. I had no idea what had happened. This must have been around the time after the bus exploded, all the way in Tavistock Square . . . when people weren't still too sure what was happening, or when they had realised the severity of it. Everyone seemed to have their mobile phones to their ears. I remember their faces, those people streaming towards me. It's funny, I never give other people on the street a second glance, I don't generally care about strangers. But that morning their faces penetrated deep inside me. Each and every one of them."

As I began to speak about what I did that morning she inched closer to me on the bench. She did this obviously and without trying to disguise the fact. It was a warmish day, and she was wearing a thin white dress that was almost transparent. When her left leg brushed up against my right it felt like it was her naked flesh touching me. She was wearing flip-flops. They were silver and black. She had immaculately painted toenails—jet black. I looked at them, each of her perfectly filed toenails. The toe immediately next to her big toe was longer, this was concurrent on both feet. Her feet were beautiful. I wanted to touch them, to plant soft, gentle kisses upon them, to caress them. To put each between my teeth, to bite down tenderly. I was aware of each of their movements: subconscious movements executed at the tips of the nerve endings.

I continued to talk about that day.

"I often think about what turns ordinary human beings into mass murderers and terrorists. There must be more to it than mere religion, fanaticism, fundamentalism. There must have been other key factors? . . . It's all so futile. So pointless . . ."

"You're wrong, of course . . ."

"Why? What makes you think that?"

"There is a point to it. Of course there's a point to it. There's got to be a point to it, otherwise . . ."

"Otherwise what?"

"Otherwise it's not worth doing . . ."

"So, you're saying there is a point to the London bombings?"

"Yes."

"A *point* to the mass murder of those innocent, everyday, working-class Londoners?"

"Yes, there has to be. Why else would they have done it?"

"But it's all so futile . . ."

"It's the banality of evil, that's what it is. Ordinary human beings doing extraordinary things. It happens. It happens in all wars . . . Human beings haven't changed, just killing machines have . . ."

"But it's wrong . . ."

"I know it's *wrong*. That doesn't mean there isn't a point to it . . ."

"What were you doing?"

"When?"

"On Thursday the seventh of July, 2005?"

"I was sleeping."

"Sleeping?"

"Yes, sleeping. I slept through the whole thing . . ."

"How?"

"I was tired. But I knew it was going to happen."

"How?"

"I just knew. It was obvious to me. It was obvious to everyone . . . I woke up that day. I don't watch much television so I didn't know immediately. It was only when I heard ladies talking about it in the newsagents that it clicked. It wasn't a shock to me. I just wanted to know who they were."

"The victims?"

"No, the suicide bombers. I knew it was suicide bombers. I wanted to see their faces—they were so young, and so . . . *extraordinary*."

"Extraordinary?"

"Yes. Who else would physically turn themselves into a machine primed for mass destruction? These are extraordinary people to me, ordinary people transformed . . ."

"But you can't say that!"

"Yes, I can. I can say whatever I want to say: the suicide bomber is an extraordinary human being. An extraordinary individual. An extraordinary machine . . ."

"A misguided individual, more like. This is nonsense."

"No. It's not. It's nothing new either."

"I don't care, it's horrific. Those people . . . the victims . . . It's all so wrong."

"But you know as much as I do why they do it."

"I do?"

"Yes. You do. There's nothing left to believe in anymore. All is fiction. Somehow, we have to invent our own reality. We have to make the unreal real. It's interesting to note that a sizable minority of extremists are recent converts. They have nothing else to do. We are empty. You know that . . ."

"Yes, I do . . . Everything is boring."

"Exactly . . ."

I felt closer to her in that moment.

It was a horrific conversation but I felt closer to her. She appeared more open to me, more susceptible to things . . . more aware. I was uncomfortable with what she was saying to me, yet she excited me that moment more than I ever thought possible. She inched even closer, whispering each word into my ear; I could feel her breath on my cheek. She was so close to me.

I was finding the urge to grab her too much.

I didn't know what to do.

My own urges for destruction had always been with me. In what seemed a harmless game to me at the time, I had, in fact, made my own homemade explosive device as a teenager. It was a crude device made from Lego, masking tape, the charcoal and oxidising agents from fireworks, and a simple fuse—I used a brand called Air-bomb Repeaters that has subsequently been banned. The idea to make an explosive device came to me in the classroom after a chemistry lesson with a teacher I hated. The idea was a bit of fun—I wasn't aware of the danger or the illegality of my game. It never occurred to me that what I was actually doing was in any way wrong. I didn't think my actions to be a deviance in an otherwise normal existence. I am in no way pathological; my conventional values and morals have always been pretty sound—but looking back it is obvious to me now that they weren't, nor have they continued to be. I don't think I understood what irony was back then, so it couldn't be described as anything other than a banal act of violence. No one pushed me into doing it—I acted alone. During that same winter the Provisional IRA were involved in their own banal acts of violence. At that time I couldn't really entertain the idea that my own efforts to create my own explosive device, no matter how clumsy, and those acts of the IRA cells in mainland Britain could in any way be related, but now, as I listened to her, her warm breath on my cheek, it all became quite clear.

I cannot begin to describe the joy I felt when I first detonated my rudimentary device. It was in London Fields behind what is now called The Pub in the Park. I forget what the pub was named then. I remember lighting the fuse and running away. The anticipation of the explosion was like an itch deep within me—completely unreachable. It seemed to take an age, but I knew not to run back to it. And then, taking me by complete surprise . . .

BANG! . . . The thing went off. It was the birds fluttering out from the trees above my head that startled me more than anything. People came out from inside the pub, too. I kept running, all the way home without looking back. When I got there I ran all the way upstairs without acknowledging anyone. I turned the TV on in my small room and hid under my duvet. I was convinced that the police would be knocking on my door at any moment. I don't think I slept that night, at least I'm not sure I did.

The following morning, quite early, I returned to the spot where I had detonated the crude device. My heart was beating, my palms sweating. I thought the police would be waiting in the foliage to pounce on me. To my amazement the explosion had left a small crater in the soft earth. I stood over it. I gasped. Red entrails and fur were scattered around it, the last remnants of a grey squirrel that had been cut down. It looked like it had been blown to smithereens. Either that or a fox had devoured it in the night. Even though I knew it was wrong I began to laugh, even though I knew this image of the dismembered squirrel would haunt me for the rest of my life it was still, up to that point, the greatest feeling I had ever experienced. I felt real. Like I had achieved something. Now, years later, it sickens me, it leaves me numb, like I can't breathe.

"There's something that's been worrying me about all this . . ."

She spoke these words to me slowly. Ever so slightly our cheeks touched, glanced, her skin as soft as a peach, warm—as I had imagined it to be. It was as if I'd known her all my life. It was if we knew each other inside out. This closeness will never leave me.

"What has been worrying you?"

"There's something about them . . ."

"Who?"

" . . ."

"Who?"

" . . ."

"Who? You can't just say that to me and stop!"

"Suicide bombers . . ."

"*Suicide bombers?*"

"Yes, suicide bombers. There's something about them . . ."

"What do you mean?"

"There's something about them that *affects* me, touches something inside of my . . . deep inside of me. I can't explain it, I can only begin to tell you about it."

"What do you mean?"

"They . . . excite . . . me."

When she said this she was so close to me her wet lips brushed against my cheek like a kiss. It sent a shiver so intense down my spine that I thought I was about to collapse. I was sure she wanted to kiss me, to hold me, to be solely with me. It felt like I had finally witnessed the reality of her, as if everything had been configuring towards this moment. It hadn't, of course, but I didn't know about that. I was trapped. I was convinced it was meant to be—that moment, those very words, that closeness, that physical closeness we were experiencing at that most naked of moments . . . And then I began to think about what she had said to me and it began to leave me cold. I had listened to that word: *excite*, with all its connotations. It rankled deep within. I didn't know what to do, I didn't know what to say. I sat there with her cheek, her lips close to mine, her breath caressing my face, the humidity of it causing the shiver within me. My body was paralysed and completely static. It took the greatest effort to move an index finger. I dared not move my head. I dared not move my face away from her. I wanted to stay like that, for that to be it, for nothing else to ever happen again. Absolutely nothing.

It's funny, life. Up until that moment I never thought I'd say something like that, let alone think it.

She became silent for some time.

It became hard for me to think of something to say. Nothing would have sounded right at that moment. I was truly empty of everything except a desire to fuck her with everything within me: every cell, every drop of blood, every ounce of oxygen fuelling each and every muscle. I wanted it so much. But I was completely powerless to make it happen. I truly was.

I looked up, momentarily alerted to something in my peripheral vision, up by the iron bridge and the Banksy graffiti. I'm sure it was a fox with a rat in its mouth. But it couldn't have been, as it was broad daylight. I didn't know much about foxes, but I was positive they kept a low profile during the day. But there it was, up by the iron bridge, running with the rat between its sharp teeth without a care in the world. I'm sure it was a fox.

"Why do they excite you?"

"It's hard to explain . . ."

"But surely you must have some idea?"

"The majority of suicide bombings are often carried out with the aid of a vehicle—a truck, a van, a car . . . or a civilian aircraft, for instance. But sometimes the suicide bombing is carried out on foot—a simple explosive belt attached to the bomber. When the bomber sets off in either their designated car, van, truck . . . *whatever* . . . when they attach their explosive belt and set off towards their pre-planned target, they are transformed, they are extraordinary . . . They are pure machine."

"But they excite you?"

"Yes . . . I'm . . . Yes, they do. They have something we don't . . ."

"What?"

"They defy death, whereas we fear it. They embrace it with open arms. For me there is something real about that. It is purely that, coupled with their use of technology and

machine, that excites me. I think of them often . . . I stare
at their faces . . . I watched the footage of 9/11 over and
over and over again when it happened . . . I still do. It was
such a beautiful image—I feel guilty for saying, for thinking
this, but I can't help it. Every time I see those images, or
any footage of a suicide bomber, I feel . . . I feel shivers of
excitement running through me."

"I don't understand that, for fuck's sake . . . Watching
those moments of massive death and destruction over and
over."

"I'm not asking you to understand. I'm asking you to
listen."

"I don't think you should tell me these things . . ."

"I'll be the judge of that. You know it's a common
misconception that all suicide bombers are poor, that they
come from impoverished backgrounds. This couldn't be further from the truth. Okay, those who detonated themselves
in London were predominantly working-class, but they
weren't poor. Most were educated, too. I often think about
them. I often watch the news reports I recorded, the CCTV
footage of them. Those extraordinary young men. I often
dream about them, their brown skin. I speak to them in my
dreams, I caress them in my dreams, I fantasise about them
during the day. Am I a sick person for doing this? Should
they be on my mind the way they are?"

"I don't know what to think. People think the strangest
things. We all wake up from dreams that make no sense to
us from time to time . . ."

"But these dreams make perfect sense to me."

"Oh . . . I . . ."

"You know, the majority of these suicide bombers show
no outward signs of psychopathology. Most people, those
not involved, have no idea of their intentions. It's no surprise to me that their relatives and friends are apoplectic

when they find out. But my dreams . . . They are increasingly sexual. But not pornographic, if that's what you're thinking. Just a tangible element of sexuality is involved. I *touch* these men, their bare skin, as they wash, as they prepare. I touch the explosives, I'm there during the bombmaking process. I help them put it together, I help them fit it into the rucksack, I help them put it on. I caress the material . . ."

"It's just a dream. It's boredom."

"It's more than that. 'Let me die with the Philistines!' cried Samson. The concept of self-sacrifice is nothing new to western society. The Christian Knights Templar sacrificed one of their own ships and hundreds of their own men just to kill twice as many Muslims. This is nothing new to us. I am not alone. We grew up with tales of the Japanese Kamikaze pilots and bombers during World War Two. Aircraft as flying bombs is nothing new to us. It was in your father's lifetime that Japanese naval officers would man and steer torpedoes; who, after aiming the torpedo at their intended target, would proceed to shoot each other dead as the machine hurtled towards its victims. We act like this is a new thing. But it's not, is it?"

"And you find self-murder exciting?"

"Yes, especially the recent bombers, more so than those who piloted the planes into the World Trade Center. The CCTV footage of the London bombers is just so modern, so normal. They looked so real, there is nothing untoward in their actions prior to the catastrophe. Then they became those extraordinary beings . . . Yet in those images there's no intimation that they were about to transform themselves. They were completely part of the ebb and flow of the city, walking into that railway station, not once looking out of place."

"You have to tell me more about your dreams . . . You have to."

She ignored me. Thinking back, it is no surprise to me that it wasn't tales of suicide bombings I was after. I simply wanted to listen to her speak intimately about those things that were hers alone: her desires and fantasies.

"Most people believe religion to be the sole cause of the suicide bombers' actions. I refute this . . ."

As she said this I saw the fox again as it rummaged for food on the other side of the canal by the iron bridge. It looked content and happy, if a little malnourished.

I pointed over to it.

"Why are you pointing over to that dog? I thought you wanted to hear more about my dreams?"

"It's a fox . . . It's not a dog . . ."

"Yes it is. It's clearly a dog."

The fox continued to look for food, oblivious to us both watching it on the other side of the canal. It was definitely a fox. I wasn't sure why she thought it was a dog. I never asked her. My hands were trembling. I wanted to put them on her thighs; I wanted to hold her. I felt foolish, like I was in some sort of dream, or caught up in some sick prank.

"You know, aside from my dreams . . . These modern suicide bombers are the dark side of the moon. We can never truly see them, be them, understand them . . . Yet they are constantly with us, only ever surfacing when the time is right. It's funny."

"What is?"

"Sometimes their actions *are* my dreams—their actions have been exiled into my unreality, my world beyond."

"Tell me about your dreams, about them, what happens in them?"

"I'm turned on, of course . . . *Is that what you want to hear?*"

"No . . . You're turned on by what they do? By their actions?"

"Just by them. They are in a room with me and I am watching them bathe and wash and prepare . . . I watch them as they calmly pack everything they need. I touch them, *stroke their skin*. I wake up every time, distressed, the sweat dripping from me, my heart beating. This dream returns to me over and over again . . . I cannot stop it . . ."

I was finding it hard to control myself as her warm breath caressed my neck, under my right ear.

I've never been able to fully remember my dreams. In fact, I was always jealous of those that could, to such an extent I would make mine up so I could be like those people who tell you their interesting and meaningful imaginings from the previous night. If I did remember my dreams they were usually images of random colours, roads, faces, sounds, and feelings. Nothing was ever coherent enough to piece together into a narrative. Over the years I began to accept these fragments as pieces of me that didn't need to be unravelled, or put back together to form a whole. The whole doesn't exist. I rather like them, my dreams, as they are: meaningless and nonsensical. I must have had dreams about people along the way. Private dreams. Dreams that I would never tell a soul. It must have happened to me, but I can't remember any of them. Even the embarrassing dreams of my teenage years have left no mark upon me—it's like they never existed.

A couple of years ago I got talking to a stranger in a pub on Kingsland Road. He had just sat himself down next to me. At first, I felt extremely uncomfortable, but his presence soon began to calm me down. I had had a busy day at work and I was trying to relax with a warm pint of Guinness. At first he pulled out a book from his bag and began to read—I have no idea what this book was, but it was thick, with a very light blue cover, possibly of clouds. Thinking back it was his movements when reading that annoyed me—the pauses, the hand on his chin, and the slight nods of the head—and I was quite relieved when he actually put down his book and began to speak to me. He had a northern accent, although it was soft and lilting and not as abrupt and thick as they can sometimes be.

"One of those days."

I glanced up from my pint of Guinness and feigned a knowing smile in the hope that that would be the end of it.

"I said, one of those days . . ."

"Oh . . . Yes . . . I suppose so . . ."

"I've given up . . ."

"Oh . . . *Given up what*?"

"Everything."

"*Everything?*"

"Yes. I've given the whole lot away."

"What do you mean?"

"My possessions. Best thing I ever did. The greatest day of my life was the day I gave away my car . . ."

"You *gave* it away?"

"Yes, to a friend. I'd had enough of it. I wanted myself back . . . my life back."

"Sounds like a good plan."

"All my life I have had this recurring dream . . ."

"Really?"

"I am alone on an island in the sun. Not even the wind to keep me company. When I was a child I used to wake up in cold sweats from this dream. But as I got older it began to make sense. It got to the point that I would lie in bed hoping that I would soon drift off to that island. And when I did I never wanted to wake up again. Waking up was just another disappointment . . . And now . . ."

"And now what?"

"And now I spend all day thinking about that island. It's all I think about. It has taken me over."

I wanted to be on that island, too—but not alone. I wanted to be on that island with her. Nothing would be able to interrupt us. She wouldn't have those dreams. She wouldn't have those thoughts. We'd exist together in sheer, unadulterated bliss.

Boredom would be ours.

She had stopped talking and was, again, staring straight ahead towards the whitewashed office block. In the silence, something about her gaze made me suspicious; I wasn't sure she had been telling the truth. It felt like she had been testing me, like I was her little pupil or something. It felt like she was revealing something to me for the very first time— something that had not yet happened, something that was obvious to her, but not yet to me. Maybe I had misheard everything she had told me? Maybe I didn't understand? The things she had said to me unnerved me; such things aren't normal. At least, I didn't think they were. But she spoke with such conviction, such vim, such heartfelt emotion that even if it was a lie, a test, I didn't care. I wanted to keep listening to her, by the canal, on the bench. It was like I was envisaging some present that could only be found in a future that could never exist . . . a future that was being reinvented by her.

I used to think about the future a lot: what it would be like, what we would be doing, what everything would look like. I used to ask anyone who would listen: what do you think the future will be like? They almost always mentioned space travel and exploration in their not too dissimilar answers; technology, computers, micro-thin TVs and other extensions of ourselves. It seemed to me the future had already been mapped out by us, like it had been invented by us, for us, that we already had a clear idea about what it was going to be like. Yet when she spoke to me that day, on the bench, it felt like something had happened, like a new future had be revealed to me, there on the bench beside the towpath and the murky water, the coots, the two swans, and the office workers. It felt like only she knew what was going to happen, what it was going to be like for us. She didn't look in the least bit surprised when I asked her what she thought the future was going to be like. It's funny, I may have imagined it, but I am certain the faintest flicker of a smile crept onto her face, a faint curl of the top lip as she turned her face towards mine. I had to ask her.

"What do you think it will be like?"

"The future?"

"Yes, the *future* . . . What do you think it will be like?"

"Well, it all depends on what you mean by the '*future*.'"

"I mean exactly that . . . *the future* . . . Everything that is ahead of us. What do you think it will be like?"

"It'll be just like it is now, only things will look different."

"What do you mean?"

"Just that. Nothing more."

She turned back to the whitewashed office block across the murky water. The canal became silent apart from a police helicopter hovering over the city towards Moorgate, hanging in the air like a dragonfly over a dead rat.

She turned to me.

"You're listening to that helicopter, aren't you?"

"Yes, I am."

"I like the sound of helicopters . . ."

"Me too."

With this, inching closer again, her breath on my cheek, my neck, she lay her head on my shoulder. A jolt of sheer electricity shot right through me. I contemplated caressing her dark hair. For a short moment nothing existed and it was the two of us. Then, as quickly as it had all disappeared, it all came back into focus: the murky water, the towpath, the discarded cigarette ends by my feet, my aching ribs, the bruises, the whitewashed office block, the expensive flats above, the iron bridge, the coots, the Canada geese, and the swans. All of it was before me as she took her head off my shoulder—like she had suddenly realised that what she was doing was wrong and unnatural—and moved away from me to the other side of the bench.

PART THREE
- weight -

- one -

For a fleeting moment, the cloud passing up above me, above the canal, above the whitewashed office block, reminded me of a giant swan floating gently across the sky. It soon shifted and morphed into something else, something unrecognisable. Yet, before it had shifted across the sky and morphed back into an homogenous shape like every other cloud, the swan figure, floating above me, opened its wings momentarily and then closed them again, slowly, like it was about to lift away. I didn't really think that much of it at the time, but now that cloud means everything to me: I imagine it over and over again. I search for them in the sky when I get the chance, but they never appear, and I know that it will never happen again, yet I still look up if the clouds are shifting at pace up above me, if I'm near a window—just in case.

I could see them in the distance, up on the walkway by the rusting iron bridge. I was sitting on the bench. I was looking at them through a gap in the privets on my left; they couldn't see me. It was the same four teenagers who had attacked me. The bright redheaded one, the tall one, and the other indistinguishable two: The Pack Crew. They were throwing things across to the other side of the bank from me, from the walkway, towards the company esplanade of the whitewashed office block, overlooking the murky water. What they were throwing looked like rocks, or possibly half-bricks. One of the teenagers was holding up his mobile phone to film the whole scene. On impact with the hardened concrete of the company esplanade, by a side entrance, the exploding rocks, or half-bricks, collided with a threatening sound: mini-explosions, the sound bouncing back off the concrete and whitewashed façade. For some reason it made me think of all those bodies falling from the World Trade Center, hitting the ground with astonishing force. I couldn't help it. The rocks, or half-bricks, were being taken from a council building site near the rusting iron bridge. Islington council were repairing a footpath, leaving huge mounds of rubble and general waste in their wake. I remember thinking why the council hadn't thought to cordon off the area so as to prevent such a thing from happening. There must have been some safety regulations for such a job? As the four teenagers continued to hurl the rocks, or half-bricks, over to the other side of the canal, another teenager appeared. He was on a motor scooter. He wasn't wearing a helmet. He must have been no older than fifteen years of age. He looked quite menacing, though. Angry, like something bad had happened. He was revving the engine over and over again. The teenager with the phone pointed it towards him, filming him, too. The engine was at breaking point, struggling with the strain of each frantic twist of the throttle—the exhaust was spitting out a thick cloud of fumes and filth. The gang surrounded him, laughing and jeering at something he had said. Then he began to accelerate forwards, bursting through and out of the huddle, up and over the rusting iron bridge at great speed, skidding to a halt at the other side, then, with skill, swinging the scooter around, low, nearly scraping the ground, to face the other way so he could ride back over the bridge again. He did this over and over again. A loud, threatening, manic figure eight. The noise was deafening. The gang, quite unperturbed, resumed their rock, or half-brick, hurling like it was their duty. Like something had told them to do it. Like automatons. The mobile phone still held aloft, still capturing the whole scene to be viewed again at leisure. The boy on the scooter continued his figure eight, revving the engine, pulling at the throttle mercilessly, his wheels burning, sliding across the rubble and bitumen. I watched them for about four minutes, until he lost control of the scooter, hitting something abruptly—probably the kerb, or some breezeblocks. He flew into the air and landed on top of the scooter, both crashing to the ground. I nearly jumped out of my skin. The gang stopped throwing the rocks, or half-bricks, and began to scream, to fall about, laughing in fits, gasping for air, holding their sides—holding on to each other. They all rushed over to the boy. Still filming it. He was lying, dazed, on the scooter. The redheaded lad switched off its engine. Then they picked the boy up. He started laughing, too, and repeatedly kicked the scooter. As soon as this began to happen the gang seemed to lose interest in the rocks, or the half bricks, and, encouraged by the tall lad with the shaven head and the teenager filming it with his mobile phone, began to collectively shout:

"Throw the fucker over! Throw the fucker over! Throw the fucker over! Throw the fucker over! Throw the fucker over! Throw the fucker over! Throw the fucker over!"

At first I thought they meant the boy who had been riding the scooter. It wasn't until I saw the gang lift the scooter and throw it—managing to beat the railings designed to stop such a thing from happening—over the side of the iron bridge and into the murky water of the canal that I realised what they meant. I watched the scooter fall. It caused a large splash, which startled some coots farther down the canal. They scattered in a cacophony of shrieks, their large feet paddling across the canal like their tiny lives depended on it. The scooter sank to the bottom of the canal. The gang, including the boy, ran away, leaving the scene in more fits of laughter. After I was sure they had gone I got up from the bench and walked over to the water's edge near the rusting iron bridge. In the middle of the canal, submerged by the murky depths, I could see the scooter lying there, settling on the uneven bed. Swirls of oil began to appear on the surface of the water, shimmering as they caught the light, spiralling in the vortex created by the sinking scooter. My immediate thoughts turned to the coots, the Canada geese, and the swans. Then I began to think about the teenager with the mobile phone.

I wondered if he had filmed them attacking me?

As soon as the ripples abated, life began to return back to normal. Four yapping coots glided across the canal by the rusting iron bridge, circling above the exact spot where the scooter had entered the murky water. One of the coots dipped its head underneath a few times before diving down to investigate the new acquisition. The seeping swirls of oil and petrol on the water's surface didn't seem to bother the submerged coot at all. The remaining three entertained themselves with a random plastic milk carton. One of the coots pushed at it with its beak a couple of times before suddenly chasing it along, shrieking to itself in what I could only imagine was excitement. Then, as if orchestrated to coincide with some secret signal, each of the three coots dived down to join the first at the bottom of the murky water in unison. I watched as a tiny pattern of bubbles formed back up on the surface. They were down there for some time before, one by one, they popped up again as the large swan, its mate, and two Canada geese elegantly paddled over to join the commotion. The four coots quickly moved on, over to the far side, beyond the rusting iron bridge. I watched the beautiful, elegant swan and its mate. He looked at me momentarily, and then looked away, heading towards the spot where the scooter lay. His long neck shot downwards, into the murky water above the scooter. The two Canada geese did the same. All three completing the investigation together. After twenty seconds or so of this they paddled away in the same direction they were originally headed, towards Hackney. I walked back over to the bench. She was there, sitting there, on her side of the bench. She was looking at me. She turned away quickly, back to the canal and the whitewashed office block.

Before I got to the canal that morning I had cooked myself a large breakfast of fried eggs, smoked bacon, fried bread, sausages, hash browns, black pudding, mushrooms, and fried tomatoes. I ate all this with four rounds of toast and a large pot of tea. I had been feeling intense pangs of hunger ever since the teenagers had attacked me. I walked to the canal that morning and I distinctly remember thinking about what I could eat for lunch. I was still digesting my breakfast but already I was thinking about lunch. I remember walking along the towpath towards the bench thinking about a huge plateful of lasagne and homemade, thin-cut chips. I couldn't help myself. It's all I could think about. Food had never really bothered me to such a degree as it did that day. I soon began to think about what I should have for dinner later that evening: I wanted duck fillets with red cabbage and cinnamon with a simple mash. I wanted to wash this dinner down with pints of Guinness—maybe four or five. Before I went to bed that evening I imagined I would have a hot steaming plate of crumpets with knobs of creamy butter, accompanied by a warm glass of milk and vanilla sugar. Then I would eventually go to bed, wake up after midnight, creep into the kitchen and devour a leftover plate of cold meats from the refrigerator.

I remember thinking to myself, as I was walking over to my bench, that I should calm down a bit—that I should snap out of it.

- two -

She was wearing a navy blue Chinese-style workers' blouse with matching three-quarter-length trousers and flat shoes. They looked like ballet shoes, although they weren't. I distinctly remember thinking she looked good. Really good. Her hair was parted in the middle, bobbed and clipped at the sides with two red hair clips. She was carrying a small handbag. As usual, she was staring straight ahead across the canal at the whitewashed office block. She yawned a couple of times, big, wide yawns, sucking in the oxygen around her, each yawn lasting an age. She didn't seem to care, not bothering to cover up her mouth. Suddenly she turned to me and began to stare. Nothing else but a long, penetrating stare, her eyes wide open. She stared at me for what seemed like a lifetime, although it was most probably only a couple of seconds. Then she turned away, back to the whitewashed office block. In those couple of seconds it felt like I had stopped breathing, or like I had forgotten how to—as if I was momentarily dead. The weight of those two seconds— the weight I felt—a suffocating weight that consumed me. For those two seconds, listless in its grip, I was dead.

And then it passed.

- three -

I wanted to shuffle up to her, to playfully squeeze her leg and make her laugh. I wanted to see her laugh so much. I knew this would be futile. I knew that if I tried such a thing it would probably be the last time I ever saw her.

Suddenly there was a strange sound, a racket and brouhaha that sounded odd. I leaned forward and looked immediately to my right, towards Wenlock Basin and Islington. Two men were staggering along the towpath. One of them—both were clearly drunk—was carrying a large bag of apples, while his companion was holding a large plastic bottle half-filled with a clear liquid. Both of the men were eating the apples, taking huge bites, finishing each in two or three gulps, then throwing the core into the canal, whilst spitting the pips to their feet and taking liberal swigs from the large plastic bottle. As they approached the bench I realised that they were both Russian, or maybe Polish. They had hard-looking, Slavic features and were dressed in thick, woollen polar neck jumpers. When they passed the bench they both turned and stopped. They looked at me and then, in unison, looked at her. Then they said something. I shrugged, not understanding. She continued to stare straight ahead. Again, they said something. I could smell the alcohol pouring from their mouths. Again, I shrugged, trying to gesticulate that I simply couldn't understand. They repeated it again, and again I shrugged. Then they offered us both an apple from the bag. I refused. Then they offered us both some of the liquid in the large plastic bottle, indicating to us that it was good, that it would warm the insides—at least that's what I understood the simple gesticulation of rubbing the stomach, executed by both men to mean. Again, I refused. They both began to laugh. I wanted them to leave us alone. I wanted them to carry on to wherever it was they were going, but they stood there laughing to themselves at whatever it was we had done—or not done—to amuse them. And still she continued to stare straight ahead, at the whitewashed office block, like they weren't even there. Like I was imagining it. Dreaming. As my right leg began to shake they both turned to start shouting at a cyclist who had suddenly sped past them a little too close for comfort. The cyclist continued towards Hackney. The two drunken Russian or Polish men began to run, to stumble after the cyclist, shouting their obscenities at him. Then, as if it was quite normal to do so, they began to throw apples in the cyclist's direction. As they did this, moving away from us, one of the drunken men fell onto the towpath, tripping over an uneven slab, still shouting and trying to throw apples. His friend helped him back up to his feet. Gradually they staggered away, soon forgetting about the cyclist. I watched them. After they had passed under the rusting iron bridge, they began to throw apples at each other, both missing, the apples hitting the murky water or smashing onto the towpath. I watched them until they disappeared out of sight. Soon their voices faded, too. And then nothing, just calm, like they had never appeared. A strange hallucination. I turned to her. She was still looking over at the whitewashed office block.

- four -

The canal was looking quite filthy; more so than usual. It was in need of a desperate dredging, but the dredgers were nowhere in sight. I thought about the grease and oil seeping into the murky water from the discarded scooter beneath its surface. I wondered what kind of effect such a thing would eventually have on the health of the swans if it was left there, underneath the murky water, ignored by the dredgers.

My gaze wandered to the whitewashed office block. The man who usually wore the slim-fitting shirts and ties was outside the office, he was leaning by a pillar on the company esplanade. He was smoking a cigarette and staring into the murky water. I watched him. I watched him because I knew now that she was watching him, too. Soon he finished his cigarette and flicked it into the canal. As he was about to turn and saunter back into the office he was joined by the woman whose desk he would always walk over to, countless times throughout the day, back and forth, back and forth. She stood close to him. He offered her a cigarette, she took it from him, he lit himself another, sharing his light with her. It didn't look like they were talking. It was hard to see, but it was obvious that they both had the same thing on their minds. She began to cough beside me, the sort of little coughs people do when they are agitated.

A military Chinook passed by over the rooftop of the expensive flats above the offices. It was quite high, nose tilted downwards, its twin rotor blades slicing through the air. I watched it. It was on a diagonal trajectory across the city—on its way, most probably, to the barracks on City Road. The HAC Grounds. I instantly thought of the makeshift morgue that was erected there the same day of the London bombings. I thought about the body parts: all that flesh and human muscle decaying under the white canvas of the marquees. The stench must have been unbearable in there. The HAC Grounds sits next to Bunhill Fields, a burial ground from the Saxon times and, since 1685, a cemetery that was once used for victims of the plague, and later on for nonconformists and some infamous writers and poets.

I used to walk to Bunhill Fields with my father from time to time. He liked to sit and feed the pigeons in there, ignoring the signs pinned to the railings urging people not to. Every time, when the feed was all finished, and I had asked him if there were really bodies in the numerous sarcophagi scattered about, he'd tell me about how the cemetery got its name. He would speak quietly, telling me how it was originally called Bone Hill and that Bunhill is a modern bastardisation of that name. He would then fall to a mere whisper as he told me about the countless cartloads—over one thousand in total—of dried bones that were taken from St Paul's charnel-house around 1549 and dumped on the boggy fen and moor that once stood on that very spot under our feet. A wondrous hill of dried bones eventually rising from the marshes, big enough to build three windmills on it—which were subsequently demolished when urgent land was needed for the myriad plague victims that had been piling up on every street corner. Each time he would end his macabre tale with the same words, a wry smile forming in the corner of his mouth: "We're literally walking over the London dead."

It would send a shiver through me, but eventually, over time, I got used to it and it soon became a running joke between us. It's funny to me now. I still think of those words most days when I'm walking through the city, to the shops, or waiting at bus stops. When I'm standing still with nothing to do or laying flat out on the grass looking up at the trees and sky, I still think of the London dead beneath my feet.

I shuffled my feet in the dirt. I began to think about those countless men who worked to build the canal. The long stretch of water making up the whole of the Regent's Canal, beginning at Limehouse Basin and incorporating Wenlock

Basin by the whitewashed office block, the 886 metre Islington tunnel, and eventually ending at Camden, where it joins the Grand Union Junction at Little Venice. It was opened in 1820. At the time, the digging of the Islington tunnel was the utmost in engineering technology and endurance. The canal's original engineer, James Morgan, designed the tunnel after a competition failed in its attempt to lure a suitable winner into designing it. Building began in 1814 and by the first month of 1815 over 140 yards of the tunnel had been built, using a technique of drilling shafts down to tunnel level from street level above. By March of the same year, 250 yards had been built and four large shafts had all been linked to the tunnel from above. These shafts served to lower men and equipment into the tunnel and also to remove earth and rock. The tunnel is more or less completely straight, a feat that James Morgan was applauded for. All 960 yards or 886 metres of it was finally completed in 1818 and cost almost £40,000 to build.

I'd read all that in an interesting article about the building of the Regent's Canal, although I now forget where I read it. It might have been in a newspaper, the Hackney Gazette, or it might have been on the internet at work when I was bored and should have been occupying my time doing something a little more productive. It was one of those stories that always sticks in your mind for no apparent reason. Like I said, I first started walking to the canal one day out of boredom—nothing else. It's not that I have ever shown any interest in canals before that day. I often wonder now why this particular story should stick in my head the way it does. It's not even a great story—it's nothing that special. It touched something within me. There's so much about myself that I do not understand. I remember reading how the barge owners used to walk their barges through the Islington Tunnel by lying on their backs on deck and literally walking along the walls of the tunnel to push it through to the other side. This antiquarian technique was called *legging*. All that toil and trouble, all that walking; it's hard to believe it even happened today. It's hard to believe the misery some people endured for us to be able to live our lives.

I wonder if all the commuters—the cyclists, the joggers, the walkers, the drifters and drunks—ever cast a thought to those who built it all those years ago. I wouldn't hold my breath.

She continued to cough. She was clearly agitated and something was obviously bothering her. She was staring steadfastly ahead to the other side of the bank at the two office workers. I watched her looking at them. At him, I realised: watching his every move, aware of everything he did. If he rolled his eyes she noticed it, if he ran his fingers through his hair she noticed it, and if he blinked she noticed that, too. It was him she was looking at, and it dawned on me finally: he was the sole reason she came to the canal, and to our bench in particular. It was him she was interested in and not me.

- five -

They must have known each other. No one would actually spend that amount of time watching one particular stranger. I watched her, trying to be discreet, although it didn't seem to matter. Suddenly, it was as if she was there standing next to them, right there across the murky water, feeling what they felt, speaking the same words, smoking the same cigarettes. She was over there with them. I watched her. It was all I could do, all I could ever do. Then her breathing became heavier, in and out, in and out. She resigned herself to the tryst across the way, out of her reach, so close she could almost touch them it seemed, on the cold concrete of the small company esplanade. I could have been sitting on a bench on the other side of London for all she seemed to care. For that moment, I was sure that I didn't exist. That I was hidden in some sort of dirty, grimy fog. I had to try and get her back to me somehow.

"Those youths were up to no good earlier . . ."

She continued to look across the murky water at the couple. I continued.

"I said, those kids were up to no good today. The same ones who attacked me that day. Do you remember?"

"Pardon . . . ?"

"Those four youths. The Pack Crew. You know?"

"I don't know . . ."

"Yes, you do. You know exactly who I mean . . ."

"What were they doing?"

"Come here, look. I'll show you . . ."

"Where?"

"*Here* . . ."

I walked towards the water's edge, near to where the scooter had been thrown in. I beckoned her over to me. She was, at first, a little hesitant, choosing to continue to stare out across the murky water at the two lovers. I beckoned her over to me again. She looked at me for a second, then paused, before looking back across the water. They flicked their cigarettes into the canal before walking back into the office. I followed him in particular; through the looming panels of glass as he made his way to his desk. Once inside the office he acted as if the tryst outside had never taken place. I looked back over to her sitting on the bench. She was looking, it seemed, at the woman as she made her way to her own desk, also acting as if the tryst on the esplanade a moment ago had never taken place. When both the man and the woman were settled at their respective desks—checking emails or whatever it was they were doing—I beckoned her over one more time. She looked over towards me. She couldn't hide her sadness. I could feel it welling up inside of her. She stood up, slowly, and walked over to me. It seemed to take forever, each footfall purposely placed in front of the other. When she eventually got to me, standing by my right, not too close—she remained silent. I pointed towards the submerged scooter.

"*There!* Look what they did . . ."

She remained silent. The handlebars of the scooter were clearly visible. I could see them. I pointed towards the scooter yet again.

"Look! See it? . . . *There!* . . . Do you see what they've done? . . ."

She took one step closer to the canal's edge.

"I can't see anything . . ."

"What do you mean?"

"I mean, I can't see anything . . . *there* . . . in the canal. I can't see anything."

"But it's obvious . . . as clear as day . . ."

"I can't see anything."

"*There! There!* The handlebars, just there, breaking through the surface of the water . . ."

"No . . . I . . . No."

"Do you think I should contact the police?"

"What for?"

"Because it's stolen. It's a stolen scooter, they dumped it here. From that bridge. They just let it drop, just like that. They were filming it all! On their mobile phone! Filming it! Into the water. No one even noticed, apart from me. No one looked up from their desks. Only me, the geese, the coots, and the swans noticed it. Where are the dredgers? Why aren't they here to clean this mess up?"

"They'll be here in time. I'm sure of that. It's their job . . . This section, this stretch of the canal must be on their agenda, their work sheet or something, if they have one, that is . . ."

"Well, they should be here. It's been days, weeks. I've been waiting for them. They should be here by now, shouldn't they?"

"I'm sure they . . ."

"All this needs to be cleaned up. Those kids can't be allowed to do such a thing. There's not even any CCTV. At least I can't see any, can you? It must be well hidden if it is there. Maybe, maybe they've been caught on that? Maybe I should speak to the security desk of that office block across the way there? Maybe they have it on film? Or maybe we can somehow get hold of their mobile phone?"

"I doubt it."

"What do you mean?"

"Why would they have their security cameras pointed at that bridge up there? Away from their own windows and doors? And who on earth is going to get their phone? *You*?"

"You're right."

"I know I am."

I felt stupid. I was truly embarrassed. I felt the sudden urge to get away, to remove myself from the canal. I wanted to take her with me.

"Are you hungry? I'm famished."

"Not really . . ."

"I know a café . . . The Rheidol Rooms . . . just around the corner."

"I know you do. You've already said. We don't need to go there right now, not now . . ."

"Why?"

"Because we're okay right here . . ."

"But wouldn't it be nice for us to just get away from here? And do something else for a change? Do something other than sit here all day long?"

"There's no need to do anything else."

"Well, I don't know about that. Something has to be done about those lads, those four . . . that gang, the gang who attacked me . . . Don't you think?"

"There's nothing we can do about them."

She began to yawn and then pick at some skin on the cuticle of her right index finger. She looked genuinely upset, like something truly tragic had happened. That same look you find on the faces of witnesses to car crashes some time after the initial shock of the event, the fatal collision, when the realisation of the severity—the actual impact—begins to reveal itself. She walked back to the bench and sat back down; I followed her. Her breathing became heavier. I shouldn't have asked her; it was none of my business.

"Do you know the man across the way?"

"*Pardon*?"

"The man from the office over there? The one who was just talking with the woman on the company esplanade?"

"I'm sorry . . . I don't know who you are talking about, I really don't. I should go now . . ."

"No, no, no . . . Please . . . *Don't* . . ."

She stood up. She was rankled by my question. I should have followed her, caught her up and apologised, but I didn't. I watched her as she walked away towards Shepherdess Walk. I turned to look inside the whitewashed office block, to see if I could see him. I could. He was sitting at his desk, busying himself with some paperwork. Transferring the information contained on each sheet—whatever it was—on to his company PC. I imagined them, the sheets of paper, to be invoices. Piles and piles of invoices, other people's information, the lifeblood, the mechanism of the times: paper converted into binary code, into html, xml— metadata. Codes. All of us programmed to shift electronic information within an abyss we cannot see, touch, or feel. An abyss of our own design, information hurtling through it, back and forth, from one place to the next and then back again in the blink of an eye. It never ends. It never stops. I watched him typing the information into his company PC: the figures, words, acronyms, and codes flashing up in appropriate boxes via the snazzy, specially designed software package used for such a purpose. His fingers danced across the keyboard as he stared into his flat-screen monitor, the artificial light emanating from it diluting his tired pupils, as he moved onto the next invoice in the pile like an automaton. I thought about the many years I had wasted processing similar information, on similar company PCs and laptops, in similar buildings. All that information I had sent into the ether, the abyss, with each click of the mouse, each press of a button and tap of a key, over and over and over again, five—sometimes six—days a week. Each click like an act of bored violence.

I shuffled to my feet. I felt like laughing: how absurd he looked. How stupid he looked sitting at his desk, processing all that information, sending it on its merry way into an abyss of our own design. How utterly stupid he looked, utterly useless, without the slightest intimation that it was all starting to slide, to slip away.

I stayed on the bench by myself for the rest of the day. I did nothing but watch him. I didn't even think that much. Not even about her. I was close to happiness—for a short while at least—and then the feeling was soon dulled by the fact that I knew it wasn't going to last.

- six -

As I was about to vacate the bench, somewhat nonplussed
and weary, ready to walk back home for food, I noticed
it on the ground, by the discarded cigarette ends, nestled
by the right-hand foot of the bench: her purse. My heart
skipped and began to pump blood faster and faster through
my veins until it felt like my head was about to explode.
It was a nondescript black purse, probably quite expensive. It was stuffed with money and credit cards. I counted
the money: £410 in total. I immediately thought of all the
things I could have bought with such an amount. Not that
I was in any desperate need for money—I had been left a
considerable sum which, if used wisely, would take care
of me for quite some time. Yet, what was she doing with
all that money in her purse? It's not that she was going
anywhere special. Surely it wasn't safe? I looked for other
things. There was an old, faded photograph. It looked like
it had been left out in the sun, or beneath a strong light.
I looked at the photograph. It was definitely her. She was
standing next to someone, a man. I suddenly looked over
to the man at his desk working through his pile of invoices,
but he had gone, his desk was empty. I was unable to com-
pare the faded image on the photograph with his bulk and
frame—not that I thought it was him. I put the money
back in the purse and pulled out two cards: a debit and a
credit card. One gold, one silver. I held both in my hands
and looked at her name. It was the same on each: _____
_____. It was an ordinary name. It suited her. If I had a
daughter I would probably want her to be called that, too.
I held the cards in my hand, staring at them. It felt like a
breakthrough had happened. I looked at the canal. The sun
must have been shining directly above me because the whole
of the canal—at least as far as I could see—seemed to be

glistening, as if it was molten rock, or mercury. It shone with a cool brilliance that I had never quite seen before. It reminded me of machinery, a conveyor belt carrying a gleaming product through assemblage towards some state of completion. I looked at it for as long as I could, for as long as it lasted, and knowing that I would probably never see such light again. Then everything turned back to how it was before I looked at it . . . the murky water, the greyness. Then, as everything changed back, as one would switch off a light in a room, I found the card.

I stared at it. It was all I could do. My heart stopped functioning, blood lay dormant within me, things stopped. I was unable to do anything with it, the card, holding it in my hand with her purse and its other contents, my body unable to register, to deal with it, a momentary lapse. The words printed upon it took a while to sink in. I cast my eyes over her address. I had her address in my hands. She was a managing director of a *web design & e-solutions* company called *telephus*. I knew all I needed to know. I knew where she lived. I held the card in my hand and began to laugh. I quickly looked in the purse for a driver's licence, but there was nothing else of any interest. I figured she must have hidden the licence somewhere, or destroyed it. But it didn't matter, the card was enough. Now I could reach her. I laughed loudly. I felt like I had made a massive step, that I had somehow become closer to her, making some sort of personal connection. My cackle startled a cyclist as he passed me by, causing him to wobble and lean to his right towards the water's edge. He stopped a couple of yards ahead and turned towards me. He didn't say anything. He shook his head as I continued to laugh. It felt like I hadn't laughed in a very long time.

I was beginning to feel at home on the canal. I was convinced that I had made the right decision to walk to it each day, instead of walking to work as usual. If I was honest, there was only one thing I really missed: the walk to work, the route I took each and every morning, before I decided to stop all of that and head to the canal. My walk to work would take me through Shoreditch Park in Hoxton. The park was originally a site of high-density housing, most of which was destroyed during World War Two, most notably in the Blitz of 1940–1. Documents record numerous V1 and V2 rockets landing in the area up until 1945. Post-war 'pre-fab' houses lasted up until the 1980s when the whole area was eventually demolished and transformed into a park. Each morning I would see the same man and German Shepherd dog out on the playing fields. The man would have a green Frisbee with him, which would hold the dog's attention, until he finally threw it up into the air, causing the dog to chase it and leap up to catch it between its jaws—which it succeeded in doing ninety percent of the time, regardless of the weather, most probably due to the expertise of the man's throw. The dog always looked so happy doing this, each morning, rain or shine, over and over again. On the few occasions that the dog would mis-time its leap to catch the Frisbee in its powerful jaws I would feel quite sorry for it, and as I would continue through the park on the path built over what was once Dorchester Street, I would become quite sure that this miscalculation would affect me some-how, my behaviour, throughout my entire working day. That German Shepherd, the green Frisbee, and the man, all combining to alter my day at any time during my short walk through Shoreditch Park each morning. A wry smile would often eke its way across my face when I thought about this on my way back home after work, walking in the oppo-site direction through the park—the dog, the green Frisbee, and the man elsewhere, oblivious to the effect they had upon me.

- seven -

That very same evening I walked to her flat on De Beauvoir Road. I remember it clearly, as if it was yesterday. I even remember the cat, on the way, that sped out from a garden on Northchurch Road, into the traffic and almost under the wheels of an oncoming car. It cowered on the other side of the road underneath a plane tree. I walked over to it, the cat, making deliberate blinks with both my eyes. I wanted it to know that I wasn't a threat. The cat blinked back, slowly. Then it walked over to me, close, executing three, maybe four, figure eights around my right leg, then stopping to rub its scent up against my shin. The cat, a tabby, made a loud noise that wasn't quite like the traditional meow of a cat—it sounded like something else, something from the woods, something wild. I knelt down before it and allowed it to sniff at my outstretched fingers. It began to lick them with its sandpaper-like tongue. Northchurch Road was silent. Even the large, early Victorian houses seemed devoid of life. It was just me and the cat. Finally, it looked up at me and slowly blinked both its large eyes before walking off into the night.

I had always wanted to own a cat. A ginger tom, to be more precise. My father wouldn't allow this, though. When asked why, he simply stated that he didn't want cats in the house. He would lie to me, proclaiming every time that he was allergic to them.

"Why don't you get a goldfish? They're more or less the same colour."

He said this to me on many occasions, but it never deterred me from wanting to own a ginger tom. So, I befriended the next door neighbour's cat—it was a ginger tom named Oscar. The name suited the cat, even though I hated a boy who lived around the corner from our house with the same name. I would feed Oscar the cat each day, ignoring my mother's protestations. I was told that cats aren't loyal, that if you start to feed a cat and the food is better than the food it already receives, the cat would walk out of its owners' lives forever. I didn't believe any of this, of course, but it sounded like a decent enough plan. I fed him everything I could get my hands on: cold meats, cheese, smoked salmon, tuna, and pilchards. Eventually, Oscar and I became inseparable, and one day Tom—the next door neighbour—noticing our new-found bond said to me, "Seeing as he spends more time with you these days you may as well have him." From that moment Oscar became my cat. I let him sleep in my bedroom without my father knowing. In fact, Oscar slept in my bedroom most nights, if he wasn't out killing, and if he did want to venture outside I would simply let him out through my bedroom window where he could hop onto the roof of our kitchen extension and then down into the garden. Most of the time he would want to stay with me and only occasionally would he stay out all night. When he did this he would return in the morning with a dead mouse for me, or a dead bird, a trophy for me to admire and accept. Then one morning he didn't return. I waited for him, imagining he was off on some mini-adventure, but when he still didn't return the following morning I began to seriously worry. I asked Tom if he had taken Oscar back in, but he told me that he hadn't seen Oscar since he gave him to me. I knew immediately that something terrible had happened to him. It wasn't until three days later that Oscar was found dead in our next-door-but-one neighbour's garden. Apparently, he'd eaten some rat pellets, or something else put out by the neighbours to repel anything feral. After Oscar's death, my father—on hearing about it—offered to buy me another "as long as it spent most of its time outside of the house," but I quietly refused.

I walked slowly onto De Beauvoir Road. Four youths on loud scooters sped past me. They made me jump. They had taken a short cut through the designated cycle routes on Northchurch Road and were probably on their way to Dalston from the direction of Islington or Cannobury. I found them quite threatening and I looked back a number of times to check that they hadn't noticed me as an easy target. Luckily they hadn't—obviously they had more important things to attend to. The streets were quiet and empty again.

It was a Victorian terrace in keeping with the area: original sash windows, pale brickwork, basement and loft both in use. All the lights were on. The house looked like it had been split into two, maybe three private flats. I had no way of knowing which one she lived in. I began to wonder if she actually lived there at all—she could have stolen the purse from someone; it might not even have been hers. It could have belonged to anyone. But then I remembered the photograph. I crossed to the other side of the road, by an old print works that had now been renovated into expensive warehouse-style apartments. At least I thought it was an old print works. I stood beneath a street lamp and two large plane trees that hung over the road, reaching upwards into the night, their branches reflecting the orange hue of the streetlamp back down onto the road. I looked up at the old print works, up at the peeling paint from its decaying, forgotten sign, the white paint fading: *Collins & Hays*. The building had huge windows, one light on in the top apartment, no sign of life whatsoever, the whole building gated and protected from the outside world.

I felt extremely uncomfortable, like I was stalking her—*I was stalking her*. I began to think that it was a bad idea

and that maybe I should go back home, sit in my chair and
do nothing. But I couldn't. I was rooted to the spot. It felt
like my body had taken charge, like it was my body that
was making all the decisions. So, I waited, there beneath the
street lamp and between the two large plane trees, shedding
their bark, bathed in the orange hue, a warm, welcoming
glow soothing my body. I looked back across the road, to
what I assumed was her flat. I looked into each window,
hoping to catch a glimpse of her. Only one window had its
original wooden shutters open. It was the main window to
the first floor, to the right of the main entrance. Even though
there was a light on inside the large, high-ceilinged room, it
was still impossible to see what was inside, especially from
across the road. Just its initial size could be estimated, and
maybe a bookshelf on the far wall, in-built, fitted. I couldn't
really be sure from my position. I concentrated, trying to
focus, to block out any interfering light that might have
impaired my view.

After about fifteen minutes, maybe more, I noticed some
movement in the first floor front room: a shadow moving
into the room. Then what I thought must have been a lamp
was switched on. It began to flicker, a metallic grey, filling
the whole room with its presence—it was obviously the TV.
I looked at the house next door to check. Its interior was
also bathed in the same flickering metallic grey, each flicker
and waver in exact synchronicity with the metallic grey light
in her room. They were obviously watching the same TV
channel. I thought about all the other houses in the area, in
the whole of London, or the entire country for that matter.

I was convinced that she was in the room, somewhere,
sitting on her sofa, watching the TV for no other reason
than there was nothing else to do—because that's what we
are supposed to do. A lower state of boredom: being bored
with something. A state of boredom that I have no interest

in. TV will not save anyone from boredom, it will only help
to prolong the inevitable. We use TV, thinking it helps us
to beat our ongoing emptiness, but it doesn't, it can't. It's a
mechanism of our own avoidance of it. Through TV we are
beaten. Its very existence is proof to me.

Suddenly the flickering stopped. I immediately looked
into the house next door: its room was still bathed in the
same metallic grey. Her room became shadows again. She
had obviously switched off her TV. This made me smile,
but I soon stopped, due to the awkwardness of my situation. Then a warm glow filled her room, a milky yellow,
like honey: it was a reading lamp in the far corner of the
room I saw when I stood on my tiptoes. The new light had
altered things, opened everything up. It allowed me a brief
view of her: she was curled up on her sofa, reading a book.
She was wearing what looked like jogging bottoms and a
white, baggy t-shirt. My calves began to ache. I stepped
back down to catch my breath. Then I stood up one last
time. There she was, before me, in her own flat.

As usual, I didn't really know what to do, or what I
was doing. The obvious thing, the thing that most people
would have done, was either to have kept the purse and its
contents, or to have handed it over to the police to sort out
its recovery. I had done neither. I was outside the owner's
house, staring in through her window, hoping to catch a
glimpse of her. But it wasn't enough, I had to do something
more. I peered into the front garden, which was neat and
well-kept. There was a garden/basement flat to the property
that I hadn't noticed from the other side of the road. The
blinds were open and I could see directly into what was a
bedroom. A man was lying on his bed—half naked—he
was a bit fat and extremely hirsute. I looked back up to
her window directly above him—it was in stark contrast. I
wondered if they knew each other, whether they exchanged

pleasantries each time they bumped into each other in
the communal garden path, or in the street. I doubt they
ever did. He didn't look like the sort, and I already knew
she wasn't.

It was at that moment that a man appeared from the
house next door. He was dressed in expensive designer
casual-wear. His garments were garish and tacky: over-the-
top lapels on his jacket, a bright polo shirt underneath, the
collars turned up, skinny trousers, so skinny it was a wonder he could move.

"Excuse me!"

"Yes . . ."

"EXCUSE ME! What are you doing just standing outside this house?"

"What do you mean?"

"I mean, I've been watching you for the past twenty
minutes. You have been acting suspiciously . . ."

"*No I've not.*"

"*Yes you have.* I've been watching you."

"Well, I don't know about you, but I can't think of any
law against me standing here in the street . . ."

"Don't take the piss!"

"I'm not."

"Listen, just be on your way, okay!"

"On my way where?"

"Wherever it is you want to go. Just not here."

"But I want to stand here."

"You can't stand here."

"Yes I can."

While he said all this he was walking towards me. Then
he suddenly slipped and fell over. He looked in considerable
pain. I helped him back to his feet. It must have really hurt
him because he remained quiet. Then he turned away and
began to slowly walk back into his house next door. When

he got to his front door he turned back towards me and stared for a long time before saying one last exasperated thing to me.

"Just go away!"

Just go away? Where? Where did he want me to go? I was outside her flat for a reason: I had her purse, her money. I was in the one place I should have been at that exact moment. There was nowhere I could have been going to—I couldn't go back to my flat or the canal now that I knew where she lived. I had *just cause*, I had something to do, a purpose. Where else could I go? Where did he think I could just potter off to?

I moved closer and looked into her flat through the window, rising up on my toes to get a better look. She was definitely in there; it was definitely her, reading, curled up on her own sofa, in her own home. The milky, honeyed glow surrounded her. I wanted her to look up and notice me, so that I didn't have to keep straining, stretching up on to my tiptoes. She seemed to be completely engrossed in whatever it was she was reading. I was aware that there was some rustling in the privets down by the small drive-way into the property. At first I didn't want to look—as tempting as it was—because I didn't want to lose sight of her, though eventually I did shift my gaze. I couldn't really make out what it was to begin with but I soon figured that it must have been a fox, or a large rat. Then I saw it: the smallest fox I had ever seen. At least I thought it was a fox. It had lost all of its fur and looked quite alien-like, its once bushy tail nothing more than a brown, leathery, thin whip-like thing. It was eating something that looked like a discarded chicken wing. When the fox eventually noticed me it stopped eating and simply looked up at me—a few seconds, if that—before it picked the chicken wing up and trotted off through a gap in a wall by the side of the house.

When I looked back up, the curtains had been drawn and I couldn't see into her flat anymore. I began to panic a little. I paced up and down, muttering to myself. I wanted to throw something at her window: a bud from a tree, a stone, something that would attract her attention enough to re-open the curtains, long enough to peek outside and see me. I began to walk away, towards Englefield Road, but I soon turned back and stood outside her flat again. The neighbour was at his window, staring over to me. He gesticulated to me that he was about to phone the police. I shrugged. I knew that his efforts to disperse me were futile, and the last thing someone like him would want would be to have the police involved. I hadn't done anything wrong for a start and he knew it. He was trying to threaten me, to appeal to what he thought might be one of my fears. In fact, the only person who had done anything remotely threatening was him, when he confronted me in the street. He was acting out of sheer vanity, ego, and embarrassment. He was a fool. He knew all too well that his actions were over the top and erratic. There was nothing he could really do. I ignored him and turned back to her window. Nothing. No lights, no movement, nothing. Not even a quiver of movement behind the curtains as if she might have been spying on me through them. The whole house was now bathed in a dark, almost menacing hue. Everything seemed closed off to me, it all seemed distant. Her life lay behind those curtains, all of it, every last morsel, all of it contained within the walls inside. There was nothing I could do. Nothing.

So I stood there, outside her flat, the two plane trees and the old print works behind me. I could have been there for hours, it didn't bother me. I wasn't interested in time, I was interested in her. I was interested in getting to her. But I couldn't. I couldn't get to her. I didn't know how to. Walking up to her door and simply knocking on it until she appeared wouldn't have been enough. It wouldn't have been enough.

De Beauvoir Road was quiet, except for the distant furore of a group of lads walking down Englefield Road, up ahead in the direction of Kingsland Road. It was a comforting racket, it made me feel warm and happy. I couldn't recall the last time I had walked drunkenly down the street with a group of friends, arm in arm, staggering, singing, and happy. I looked off to where De Beauvoir Road joined up with Englefield Road, by the small roundabout, as the group of lads were passing. I could see there were six of them in total. Two of them were wearing Arsenal Football Club shirts—they must have been warmed by the booze, as it was quite cold to be wearing just a football shirt. They must have been to the match, I figured. I had lost track of the time. I suddenly realised that before I started walking to the canal I would have known whom Arsenal would have been playing, because I was interested in things like that back then. Things like football matches back then actually mattered to me. The days following my first encounter with the bench and with her could never be the same. I was distinctly aware of this. Standing there back under the plane trees, it rattled inside me like something loose within a wind-up clock. Some cog or regulator that had somehow worked itself free from the rest of the tightly tuned mechanism, yet still not integral enough to bring things to a halt.

Little by little, it began to dawn on me that my actions were proving to be quite futile. I was caught inside something that I didn't quite understand. The very fact that I was standing outside her flat in the street was testament to this. The thought that she probably wouldn't have cared if she had known I was there was proof enough. But there I remained, outside her flat. My eyes felt heavy and I strained to keep them open. I folded my arms and leaned back against one of the plane trees. All that concerned me that night was her presence, behind those curtains—the eeriness that I somehow felt close to her.

- eight -

I must have fallen asleep, as when I next looked up the streets were deserted and there was no sound whatsoever, not even the sound of traffic in the distance, or an aircraft or helicopter overhead. It must have been the early hours in the morning. It was a miracle I hadn't fallen over. I was cold. Maybe it was around three or four a.m., I don't know. How could I have fallen asleep? It didn't quite add up. I was standing up, for a start. Surely people would have walked past me and disturbed my slumber? I couldn't believe that I had fallen asleep, but I realise that I must have done. I looked up to her window. All the lights were on—not just the reading lamp, all of the lights—in every room. Her curtains were wide open and she was standing there, at her window, looking directly at me. I shivered with fright. She looked like a ghost: ghoulish and vacant. It took a moment to sink in: she was completely naked. I began to shake quite uncontrollably. I should have walked away, but I didn't. I walked towards her flat instead. As I walked towards her she put her hand on the windowpane, palm out, her fingers spread. I tried to ignore her medium-sized breasts and thin strip of pubic hair but I couldn't. I needed to get inside of her flat. Inside her. I opened the wrought-iron gate and walked into the small garden. All the basement lights were out, only the fierce light from her window poured down upon me—the shadow cast from her naked, stoic form spread itself suggestively up towards the neighbour's wall at an obtuse angle, darting outwards, past me, through me. I looked up to her silhouette above me, hanging over me, as I walked up the steps to her front door. My skin felt like it was bubbling. I began to sweat, it poured down my forehead, and down the small of my back, I was completely and utterly outside of myself. I banged on her door, I shouted out to her. But she wasn't there. I stepped back, retreating back down a couple of steps. The curtains were firmly shut. It was as if she had not been there at all, at the window, staring at me—but she had. I saw her, I'd looked into her eyes. I knew that I hadn't been hallucinating, that I wasn't insane. I stepped back up to her door and began to thump it again. This time I shouted her name—or what I understood to be her name, the name I had found on the business card in her purse. I shouted this name over and over again. Nothing. My voice echoed in the street. Eventually, a dog started to bark in the distance. I knocked on her door three more times before walking away. I held her purse in my hand; I wanted to hand it to her, to make sure that it was returned to her safely.

I crossed the road and stood back under the street lamp between the two large plane trees. I began to think about what I should do next while looking at the peeling, textured bark on the plane tree to my immediate left. I didn't want to do it but something compelled me to walk back up to her front door. I began, as I re-crossed De Beauvoir Road, to contemplate making contact with her. I had two choices: either smash the door down or keep banging until she reappeared. I chose neither. I realised my actions were futile, so I posted her purse through her letter box—its contents intact—and walked away, back to my flat, trembling and in silence.

- nine -

It happened on the following morning: I caught the elongated drone of jet engines whining down into gear, Pratt & Whitney PW 4062 twin turbofans, slowing down into an elongated yowl, like a yawn. I looked up to see the Boeing 767 200s hanging there in the grey sky above me like a still life, motionless—a nanosecond of beauty before it began to move again. It was a sight I have never tired of seeing, only this time it made me feel dizzy, like I was about to fall from a ladder, or how I imagined it to be walking over an unsafe bridge without a handrail. Everything, including me, was in the grip of gravity, everything was being pulled down towards a dense centre, towards our centre, while this Boeing 767-200s, hanging up there in the grey sky above me, seemed, if only for a fleeting moment at least, to be purposely defying all that. It was odd that such a plane— basically, a hunk of metal—should be up there above me as the American Airlines' Boeing 767-200s were usually used for American internal flights only, from Boston to L.A.— that sort of thing. It was as if it was lost, or had been blown off course, caught, a lone twin engine staggering across the Atlantic, all 48.51 metres of it. Again, I thought of each plane hitting the first and then the second tower of the World Trade Center all those years ago: the first, a Boeing 767-223ER, crashed into the north tower killing all ninety-two people on board, the second, a Boeing 767-222 crashed into the south tower, killing all sixty-five people on board. I wondered how many people were sitting on board the Boeing 767-200s above me. I wondered who they might be, what they could see. The whole of London was a sprawling mass below. I wondered what they might have been thinking about, at that moment, up above me. I wondered if they could feel gravity's pull—like I could.

My moment with the Boeing 767-200s was broken by its twin engines slowing down again, both engines as big as those used on 747s, howling across the grey sky. Things began to start moving again, as the bulk of the aircraft floated across my line of vision, arching, banking above the city and the canal. I watched as it continued across the grey sky, like I had done so many times before, as it followed the Thames below, westwards towards Heathrow. Its fuselage looked like a shark—they always do—the grey sky like the water's surface up above it, the shark heading towards its prey. The pilots in the cockpit monitoring each movement and each minute reaction to the air currents and thermal pockets up there, preparing for their landing procedures, the same routine acted out each day, each flight, simulated and real, above the skies of London—a continued defeat of gravity.

Pretty soon another plane, an Airbus A320, appeared where the first had floated into view, above the city, slightly to the left of the previous plane's flight path. I watched this one, too. It felt like I could do this all day long, until the flight paths changed for the evening. I wasn't sure if anyone else felt quite like this, but I really hoped there was someone who did. The thought, the same thought, of spotting a plane at that precise moment: the moment it is free, stationary, free from gravity's centrifugal pull.

It made me feel like laughing—that those fearful of flying, unaware of this continuous victory, unaware that they are, in fact, part of something spectacular, within something remarkable, were captured everyday in the sky by people like me, if there are any, down below, wishing they were up there, with them.

It felt peculiar wanting to laugh to myself, on my own, my body beginning to shake.

It felt really strange.

- ten -

For some reason I knew she wasn't going to appear at the bench that day, but I waited patiently for her anyway, all day long. I sat there and watched the two swans. I watched the male take off and land over and over again. He did this maybe eight or nine times during the course of the day. It was, at times, an impossible-looking procedure, and there were moments—his mate watching too—when I thought that he wasn't going to make it, and sometimes I felt like the stretch of canal wasn't long enough for the feat. At about the second take-off I noticed, directly ahead of me, the man in the whitewashed office block watching the swans, too. He was wearing his grey cardigan again, with a bright red tie and white shirt. He was sitting, his chair turned to face the canal, away from his desk, looking directly at the swans. He seemed transfixed. He watched, along with me, as the male swan, again, prepared for take-off.

I was concerned. The dredgers still hadn't come and I was worried that the swan might injure itself on a discarded beer can, or, distressingly, the dumped scooter lurking underneath the water's surface, as it raced across the canal, ready to take to the air. The dredgers should have been there long ago. It was getting quite messy out there, things needed to be shifted, to be taken away.

I continued to watch the swan each time it prepared for take-off. Before he finally took to the air he would gracefully float, paddling towards the far end of the whitewashed office block, away to the right of the bench, down the canal, away from me and the man, about thirty metres or so towards Wenlock Basin. There he would turn to face the rusting iron bridge in the distance to my left. Here it would almost look like he was mentally preparing for the feat that awaited him: staring straight ahead, like an athlete readying himself for the long jump, before slowly beginning to move forwards, quickening his pace, half lifting himself out from the murky water, impressively, with extreme determination, somewhat at odds with his natural stoic self. He must have weighed about fifteen kilos out of the water. He, the cob, was big. I watched as he gained speed, passing directly by me, almost running, his huge, white wings spread out, flapping. The feathers splayed, like an aircraft's slats and flaps, and then, his feet still frantically running, though almost as if in slow motion, the swan lifted into the air, after passing underneath the rusting iron bridge. Instinctively missing any of the assorted debris in his path. I watched him gain height, tucking in his legs snugly, and bank back towards the bridge and bench, high above, heading west, following the canal. It was a magnificent sight—like watching the Boeing 767-200s bank across the London sky. I felt that something great had been accomplished. I wanted to shout to him, to congratulate him on his feat. It felt like something more important than life or death.

It was an awkward procedure: the three of us—me, the man in the whitewashed office block, and the swan's mate—watching this beautiful creature lifting itself out of the murky water and up, away from us, into the air. It seemed to take an age, and at one point during take-off, before it eventually became airborne, it looked like it wasn't going to happen. But it did; I saw it with my own eyes: the swan, its beautiful white wings exercising each muscle at full stretch, arched, flapping, lifting its bulk into the air, slowly, forcibly, with concentration, like its sole being depended on it, a complete dislocation with the earth, with the ground beneath my feet.

I looked over to the whitewashed office block. The man was looking up at the swan, too, and although the swan was now out of my line of vision it was obvious that he could still see it. The man remained there, his chair facing the canal, looking up at the swan until it disappeared from his own line of vision, then he turned around, wheeling his chair back to his desk to resume his tasks.

I noticed a rather odd mound of twigs and debris, earth and rubbish near to where the swan's mate was still resting. I figured this mound to be their nest. It was much larger than anything the coots used. A nest of canal detritus. There were no signs of any signets, but there must have been some on the way. I hoped that there were some on the way. A bird of such splendour and monogamy deserves something in return.

I turned my attention back to the air: the swan in flight, the huge whiteness of it, the hulk of it returning to the canal, its fine wings, feathers splayed as it descended back towards the murky water, stalling against the air, returning back, back to its mate, embracing gravity again.

The swan finally landed. I looked over to the white-washed office block: he was working, head down, still at his desk, staring at some papers, some files. He had forgotten all about the swan, the spectacle. He was back at his desk. Working. He had missed it.

- eleven -

It had felt like an entire age had passed me by since I wrote my letter of resignation. I still didn't regret it as such, but I wished I had written it better. Its composition was far too rushed, too abrupt, too haughty. It wasn't really me. I wish I had explained things better. Clearer. I tried to re-write the letter many times one afternoon, but the page remained empty. It was an impossibility to me. It felt like my arm, my right arm—I was writing this letter, or attempting to write this letter, in longhand, in a spiral notebook—consisted of lead, pure liquid lead running through its veins, filling up its bones instead of marrow. I couldn't even lift it to the page, I could just about grasp my black Pilot V5 Hi-Techpoint 0.5 pen. That was it. Nothing. No matter how hard I tried to re-write that letter I failed to do so. It was a complete impossibility.

PART FOUR
- gravity -

- one -

I was unaware of what time it was in the morning; time just
seemed to be dragging me along. I was walking to the canal.
I couldn't remember what day it was. It was probably mid-
week. The light was odd, a mixture of shadow and slanting,
piercing shafts of yellow. Rainclouds were forming. Nonetheless, those who were walking to work along the towpath seemed to possess a far more agreeable and upright
gait than usual, despite the ominous gathering above. Gone
were the bent backs, the downward glances and dishevelled
postures. Now there seemed to be direction and purpose
to their collective footfalls. Even the cyclists seemed more
positively energised, thanking me for moving aside as they
trundled by, actually adhering to the suggested *two tings*
rule. I walked along, observing the reflections in the murky
water, until I heard a helicopter overhead. I looked up to see
it hanging there in the distance, above Islington. It was dragging beneath it a huge advertising banner for some airline. I
tried to measure the size of the banner by using the façade
of a block of flats to my right as a gauge, but it proved to
be impossible due to the differing perspectives. I was finally
happy with it simply being huge: a huge advertising banner

hovering up high above me. Happy that I was untouched by it, that it wasn't interfering with me, that it was, simply, distant. Below me, by my feet, I could hear the canal lapping against the concrete bank.

- two -

I noticed it immediately and felt crushed. I felt like an insect must feel: its life being squeezed through its exoskeleton underneath the weight of a boot, then consciousness slowly fading down into the dirt and the filth. It was quite hard to fathom what was happening at first glance. All I knew was that the bench was no longer there.

In its place stood a man-made wall, consisting solely of large wooden boards. It stretched as far as I could see, all along the right-hand side of the canal. A lone construction worker was painting it white.

I wasn't sure what to do. I didn't know where to look. I couldn't sit on the bench, as the bench had disappeared somewhere behind the wall—if it even existed at all anymore. I looked to where the bench used to be, or where the wall now occupied the space in front of it, towering over me, all eight or nine feet of it. It didn't make sense to me. I looked for her. I couldn't see her. There was no sign of her at all. I stood by the wall. I felt stupid. I was highly visible against it. It loomed above me. It made me feel small—something I'm usually not aware of. My right leg began to shake. I didn't know what to do. I was feeling like a house cat must feel when walking into a recently refurbished home.

I rested the back of my head against the newly painted wall, not really caring if it was still wet. I noticed the workman who was painting it down the far end, towards Islington, looking at me for a short while before putting his wet roller back up to the wall to continue his laborious chore. He must have momentarily wondered what I was doing there, leaning against his newly painted wall for no apparent reason. I turned fully to my right, putting my right eye to the wall so I could look all the way along it towards Wenlock Basin and the trendy developments there, the Victorian warehouses and Georgian rooftops peeking above the trees of Islington in the distance. It seemed that about four cranes had sprouted up from the earth over night, each assigned to a specific purpose, each lifting and moving things up into place. The murky water was shimmering in the odd light, with dark patches of black cut and spliced into geometric patterns that moved forwards with purpose, mirroring the progress being developed on either side. Buildings that had once dwarfed the surrounding area were soon to be dwarfed themselves by the newer gleaming structures appearing like fungi from any available space. The canal was disappearing, its bridges and towpaths would soon be widened and extended, the towpath would morph into an 'urban space', the bridge into a resting point, a platform to view the new lifestyles on show. I hated it all. I really hated it all. And the sad thing, the thing that began to rankle deep within me, was that I was powerless to stop it.

Gradually, I noticed two colourful signs that had been riveted onto the freshly painted wall. I could see that both signs were repeated further along the wall at exactly the same height, maybe four or five times in total. The first of these signs read:

creatingthrivingcommunites

It was written in an everyday font like Helvetica or Impact, all the letters lower case and set as if it was one continuous word. But in case anyone thought it *was* one word, the designers of the sign had coloured the word *creating* in green and the word *thriving* in red; the word *communities* was left black. I figured that each of these colours must have been deliberated over for some time by whichever design team worked on this sign. I figured that the word *creating* coloured green must have been designed that way in order to symbolise an organic and eco-friendly environment and the word *thriving* coloured red must have been designed to symbolise vibrancy and action. I felt that the word *community* was left black because the new, young professionals were yet to move into the proposed properties that were about to be built, so there was no way to judge which colour might represent them. The second sign, which was much bigger—an obvious *death knell* to the existing residents of the Packington Estate—read:

Phase 1 will include 127 new affordable homes for existing residents in a mixture of 1, 2 and 3 bedroom apartments in two 6-story blocks overlooking the Regent's Canal and a terrace of 3, 4, 5 bedroom houses.

The second sign was more practical; there was no colouring; there was no need for it to dazzle any passing pedestrian. It merely conveyed the inevitable. I looked at the top of an existing block of flats from the Packington Estate. No matter what the new sign said, these new flats were not going to be affordable to the average resident of the estate. I wondered what they thought about all this. I wondered if the designers of the sign had thought about how all this was impacting on the original residents.

I waited for her. I knew that she would eventually appear; I was completely and utterly sure of it. I started to whistle. I forget what song it was that I actually began to whistle but it was something popular and melodic. I didn't care who could hear or see me standing there, whistling as loudly as I possibly could. Eventually two coots passed me by, both looking at me. I crouched down towards them both, stepping forwards to the edge of the canal. The water around them was filthy. I could smell it. The stench enveloped me. I have never smelt anything quite like it since. It was a seriously disgusting smell, like something was decaying. Like the whole canal was dead. The two coots soon became bored with me when they realised I had no food and they paddled away. I stopped whistling. I watched the two coots, their large feet hidden beneath the sickening slurry. For the first time in my life, at that exact moment, crouched down by the canal, I realised that things—stuff, matter, everything—was absolutely pointless. Everything should be left alone. Nothing should be touched. Because even the dredgers were powerless to halt such unremitting decay.

- three -

It began to rain. A light, greasy drizzle. It didn't bother me. I was waiting for her. Suddenly, I heard a strange noise: shouting, instructions, and machinery. It came from the direction of the lock at Wenlock Basin. Pretty soon I saw it: a dredger. It was heading my way. A medium-sized, three-man contraption. I began to laugh. At the same time I wanted to shout out, "*Too late! Too late! Turn back! Turn back!*" But I didn't. I wanted to avoid any kind of scene. So I allowed the dredger and its team to slowly, achingly move towards me.

They were cleaning up the silt and sludge, the thick mud from the murky depths of the canal. Anything else they retrieved up from the bottom must have felt like a bonus compared to the shit-coloured mess they sucked up. If anything was found, a portable TV, a mobile phone, or an old boot for instance, one of the three operators would holler at the other two in excitement, each of them helping him to drag the item into their cabin. I looked at the slurry that was being sucked up from the canal. I wanted them to leave it where it was. After longing for the dredger to turn up all this time, I simply wanted it to turn around and go away. They were changing things, disturbing everything. I wanted to tell them that nothing needed to be changed. To leave it there to fester at the bottom of the canal.

I watched as they reached the rusting iron bridge, finding the submerged scooter with no trouble at all. They attached the small on-board crane to it, and the mechanised arm lifted the scooter out from the murky water with considerable ease, separating it from the mud and shit and discarded plastic bags clinging to its handlebars and wheels. It looked like a monster from the deep, like it was about to come back to life and terrorise us all. The dredger team lifted it onto their barge and looked it over, pleased with their find, hoping that it could somehow be salvaged.

I stood by the wall, where the bench used to be. I watched the dredger. It was called *The Ducketts*. I had no idea what that meant, but I liked the name nonetheless. I wasn't aware, until that moment, that dredgers had official names, much like a train or a civil aircraft. It had a blue cabin at the far end, with a large lowered deck for the retrieval of debris, its outer rim flat so the operators could walk around it. At the opposite end to the blue cabin was the crane that was used to lift heavier things that had become embedded in the slutch up and out of the water. The dredger was near-filled to capacity, and I remember thinking that it was a real feat of engineering that such an awkward looking piece of machinery could actually float.

I had been waiting for this pathetic moment since I first walked away to my bench, and even though the dredger had finally appeared I still didn't feel that everything I wanted—the cleaning of the muck and slutch and filth around me—would ever happen. Nothing appeared. All this waiting. Nothing but here. Endless here.

- four -

Again, I put my head up to the wall to look down along it, to follow its line, this time with my left eye, towards Hackney. That's how I saw her appear, walking towards me. She was looking up at the sheer size of the wall, looking up at it as she walked along. Slowly. She seemed in a trance, enveloped in a thick miasma. It was as if she was expecting every minute detail of the new structure, every workman's nail, every angle and board. I watched her all the way, my head resting on the cold wood, all the way to me—or where the bench, our bench used to be. She traced her fingertips along the smooth surface of the wood. She was still caressing it when she finally stopped beside me.

"It's all gone then . . . ?"

She uttered these words quietly. I knew instantly what it was she actually meant. Our space had shifted. We felt uncomfortable. Awkward and mawkish. We felt exposed. Revealed. I drew my eyes up to look at her fully, lifting my head back off the wall. I felt embarrassed. I answered her.

"They've put it up because of us . . ."

She ignored me, staring up at the wall; then turning to look over to the whitewashed office block . . . before eventually turning back to me.

"This is no good."

"What? Here?"

"Yes. *Here*. It's no good anymore."

"Well, shall we go and get something to eat? I know a café not far from here."

"Yes. I know you do. Okay then."

"Pardon?"

"*The café.*"

I was quietly surprised by her answer. My legs felt like lead. I tried to say something to her. I tried to say, "I've been waiting for this . . ." But I somehow couldn't form the correct movements and positions with my mouth, it opened, but simply wouldn't do anything. Nothing seemed to work. Eventually I managed to mutter, "Yes."

So we walked along the towpath. Towards Islington. Towards the Café. The Rheidol Rooms. I felt like an automaton walking along with her. I remember gliding along like I was a machine on autopilot. Like it had all been pre-programmed pre-route.

- five -

As we walked along the towpath a gaggle of Canada geese joined us, paddling alongside at exactly the same pace, their heads bobbing back and forth in motion. There were seven in total. I counted each one to make sure. Then I noticed that one of them wasn't a Canada goose at all; it was a smaller, stockier breed, sporting a bright orange bill. She, or he, looked happy, not caring about being different, not bothering about its individuality, happily paddling along. They continued alongside us until we reached Wenlock Basin, where they turned left, away from us, towards a group of people eating sandwiches by a bench below the expensive flats on the other side of the basin.

We walked in silence. I was thinking about the wall, about what they were building on this side of the basin: more expensive flats. People would be marginalised, people would be removed, those who couldn't afford to stay. It didn't seem fair. It didn't seem right. All of a sudden it hit me: it felt odd, slightly disingenuous even, that she would join me for some lunch, something that she had vehemently resisted doing with me so many times before.

- six -

The café was empty. We walked inside and took a seat at a small table for two by the window. A bored-looking wait-ress looked up from her fingernails and walked over to our table. She stood over us, waiting for us to speak. The taint of fried egg and chip fat followed her. I liked her, there was no fuss about her persona; she was plain and simple. She existed and that was enough, there was no need for any-thing else because everything else was superfluous to her. I raised my eyes. I could see straight up her nostrils.

"I'll have a black coffee and . . ."

I turned to my companion. She was looking at the menu, furrowing her eyebrows into a tight V. Then she looked up, smiling.

"I'll have a hot chocolate and a baked potato with chili, please . . . May I have lots of butter on the potato?"

The waitress shrugged, as if to imply that ordinarily she wouldn't give out extra butter to customers. Then she turned to me, but I'd been observing them and wasn't prepared.

"Are you not eating? I thought you were hungry."

"I don't know what to have . . ."

"Have the same as me . . ."

"Okay, I'll have the same again, please . . ."

"Extra butter for you, too?"

"Er . . . Yes, please."

The bored waitress walked away to the kitchen. As I was about to open my mouth to speak, two more people walked into the café. A man and a woman. I didn't recognise them at first, probably because it was the first time I had seen them up close. But after a moment it hit me—it was them, the couple from the whitewashed office block. The same man and woman who had been smoking out on the company esplanade. The man in the tight shirts and cardigans, the woman who sits at the desk that he walks back and forth to throughout the working day. It was definitely them. They eventually took a table opposite us after looking up at the menu boards above the counter. They sat down after he carefully removed her coat for her, smiling, giddy, happy, sitting close together, huddled.

She wouldn't look at them. She stared down to her feet. I knew that she knew who they were. She had seen them enter the café and eventually recognised them as I had. A deathly silence descended upon our table. I didn't know what to do to defeat it. I felt completely powerless. She was hunched over, staring down at our table, at her feet. Something to concentrate on, something to divert her eyes and mind away from the couple from the whitewashed office block sitting directly opposite us, close enough to hear, to smell. I tried to listen to what they were saying but they were purposely talking in whispers, sensing the quiet, aware that they could be heard, lending the situation the feeling that it was some sort of clandestine tryst.

Suddenly the man leant over their table and kissed her. It was a lingering, open-mouthed kiss on her lips, intimate and sensuous. There was no movement in front of me, although I could detect a fierce rage building inside her. She definitely didn't want the man and woman there, at the table opposite us, and she obviously didn't want there to be any physical contact between them. She knew who they were, or at least him. It was her sole reason for sitting on the bench each day. Her sole reason: him.

I tried to gain her attention by pointing to a cat out through the window. It was crossing the road from the opposite side where the Duke of Cambridge pub was.

"Look! A cat using a zebra crossing! How clever!"

". . ."

She shrugged. She did it without looking at me. Then she yawned. I began to speak some more; I couldn't handle the situation, the silence. This wasn't how I had envisaged it to be.

"What do you think they're building?"

She looked up immediately. I asked this already knowing the answer, but it was all I could think of to ask her.

"*Who? Them?*"

She raised her eyes towards the table opposite.

"No. No. No. Not them . . . No . . . The space. Where our bench used to be. What do you think they're going to be building? The health centre will be knocked down and everything . . ."

"*Building?*"

"Yes. Where our bench used to be . . ."

"Flats."

"Do you reckon?"

"I don't care, to be honest."

"Oh. Why?"

"It's a pointless and boring question."

"Oh."

"*I really don't care.*"

She continued to look downwards, towards her feet, the floor, a speck of dust. She looked uncomfortable, as if she didn't want to be recognised. The man and woman were laughing, sharing a secret joke or something. They were sitting closer to each other, and he was stroking her cheek with the back of one hand. She was blinking, blushing a little, not coquettishly, but knowingly, as if they had planned something devious together. The woman was wearing a tight black skirt and black, thin tights that were thin enough to give a hint, a sniff of pale flesh underneath. She was almost bursting out from her expensive-looking white blouse. She was clicking the heel of her right stiletto on the tiled floor—like an old clock ticking down the hours. In the silence that had now descended upon the whole café, her clicking heel was all that could be heard.

Click.

Click.

Click.

Click.

I noticed that my own right leg had begun to shake furiously—as if in synchronicity with the sound of her heel. I tried to stop it but I couldn't. Then our food came, the bored waitress almost dropping each plate onto the table. I stared at my plate of food. I couldn't eat it. I looked up and she was tucking in, eating it like it was her last ever meal.

"You're hungry."

"Yes."

"Are you in a rush?"

"Yes."

I took my knife and fork and dug into the hot steaming potato covered in the thick, indistinguishable chili. I swallowed it quickly. It was way too hot for the roof of my mouth. On any other day this would have been a great little meal and

I'd have probably wolfed the whole lot down, but the sudden appearance of the man and woman from the whitewashed office block had put an abrupt halt to any such thing.

His hair was perfectly groomed in that ruffled, just-got-out-of-bed look that seemed popular with males of no imagination who still followed the fashions. His shoes looked expensive. There wasn't a blemish on his face. It was a happy, good-looking face, contained and unaware. She had recently dyed her hair it seemed; it looked healthy and in vogue. By her clicking heel was her expensive-looking bag—large, garish, open and stuffed with three thick, glossy fashion magazines. She looked happy, too.

- seven -

"Why aren't you eating your food?"

Her plate was empty and she was looking directly at me, holding her mug of hot chocolate in her cupped hands.

"I don't know . . . It's just that . . ."

"That what?"

"Well, that as soon as those two people walked in . . . that man and woman . . . something changed."

"*Something?*"

"*You.* You changed, you turned inwards . . ."

"Why would those two people affect me?"

"I don't know. You tell me."

"There's nothing to tell . . ."

"*Yes, there is.* But you explain things only when you want to, it always seems . . ."

". . ."

I was beginning to feel quite angry. I wanted to shout something out. I wanted to shake her.

She began to yawn, quite openly, looking back down towards her feet, avoiding the man and the woman on the table opposite.

I have often thought that cafés are strange places— especially if you frequent them alone. A kind of nothingness can be created, seated as you invariably are at your pre- ferred table by the window, watching the world pass you by outside, or the rain trickle down the pane. It is as if you are floating, completely suspended in nothingness.

- eight -

They began to kiss again. This time for longer and with added passion. Both continued in a world of their own mak- ing. A world there, opposite us, close enough to touch, or disrupt. The kiss lasted for minutes; it was quite uncomfort- able to watch, but it was impossible to ignore. It felt awk- ward, like we had all walked in on a private moment.

Click.

Click.

Click.

Click.

It was at that moment that she began to sob in front of me. Silently. Her shoulders shaking. The tears streaming down her cheeks, hardly showing any emotion. I tried to reach out to her, to touch her hand, but she recoiled, as if my mere touch would harm her.

She allowed the tears to fall, smearing her mascara, trickling down each pale cheek. I wanted to wipe them away, but I knew there was nothing I could have done to help her.

- nine -

Everything was beginning to make me angry. It should have been me on the table opposite, not with the woman he was with, but with her. I should have been there, doing those things, the same things as he was with her.

Her tears wouldn't cease, and her silence somehow made them seem all the more significant—like she was crying for everyone.

I have never been able to handle the tears of other people. I have walked out of rooms when I shouldn't have done as close friends of mine have allowed the tears to fall from their eyes in front of me. I have asked family members to stop crying at funerals. It's not that I am against emotion or the outpouring of sadness. It's the physical secretion, the physical act, the physical act of expelling something from deep inside. It's like the force of gravity has pulled each tear from within the body, back out, down towards the earth where it belongs. It's the constant reminder of the weight that envelops us all—the return to nothingness. To dirt.

"Why are you crying?"

". . ."

"*Please*, why are you crying?"

". . ."

"*Please, answer me . . .*"

". . ."

The other couple had stopped kissing and had started to tuck into their own food after the bored woman had interrupted them with it. After each mouthful they would stop to giggle and whisper. I don't think they even noticed us sitting opposite. I don't even think they knew we were there.

"*Please*, why are you crying?"

". . ."

"What's wrong?"

" . . . "

"*Please*, I'm concerned . . . *Are you okay?*"

" . . . "

She wiped away the tears from her eyes. She looked up at me, she looked over at them, all the while wiping the tears away, the woman's heel still clicking.

Click.

Click.

Click.

Click.

I couldn't really think of anything to say. It seemed impossible to say the right thing. I wanted them to leave, to leave us alone. Suddenly, she turned to look at me.

"I'm sorry."

Before I could reply, before I could blink even, she rose from her seat and walked over to their table. She addressed only him, ignoring the woman, without even as much as a derisory glance towards her. The man and the woman stopped what they were doing and both looked up at her simultaneously. The man had a nonplussed look upon his face, probably thinking there was a problem with his order or something.

She addressed him only.

"Do you remember me?"

There was a long pause.

He looked at the woman next to him, then back at her, then back at the woman. He looked nervous, rubbing his thumb into the palm of his hand. The woman's eyes began to narrow and her whole face started to contort. He looked back up at her.

"Er . . . I'm . . . afraid . . . I'm afraid I don't, sorry. Er . . . Have we . . . Should I?"

"*You tell me.*"

"I'm sorry, I've never seen you before in my life. I fear you may have mistaken me for another person, someone else in your life . . . I'm sorry."

"You're *sorry*?"

"Yes."

"You're *sorry*? That's all you can say? *Sorry*? Don't you remember me at all?"

"I'm sorry, but no, I clearly don't. I clearly don't remember you from anywhere, I have never seen you before in my life. Now, we were having a private conversation. I'm sorry, but . . ."

"So, you just want to leave it like that?"

"If you don't mind, I'd rather, yes."

"No. I want you to tell me who I am. I want you to tell me who I am. You have to tell me."

"I'm sorry, but I seriously have no idea. Can you please leave us alone now?"

"*No*. Do you not remember who I am?"

"No, *I do not*. I have never set eyes on you before in my entire life. You have clearly mistaken me for another person. *Please leave us alone.*"

I was beginning to feel more than ill at ease with the whole situation. The bored waitress behind the counter was leaning on her elbows, chin in palms, looking over toward them, smiling, happy to be watching the burgeoning spectacle before her, happy, at last, that something was eventually happening that day. I remember uttering the word 'no' twice, but it went unheard in the ensuing mêlée. I watched as she threw the glass of water over him, the plates crashing to the floor, breaking into shards and fragments, scattering across the tiles into far-flung corners of the café. The blonde woman's deafening scream nearly burst my eardrum. The man, now soaked, his white shirt sticking to his skin, rose to his feet and pushed her to the floor. She immediately jumped back to her feet and continued her attack, swinging for his face, trying to pull his hair and scratch his cheeks. The other woman began to fight back, too, holding her, leaning over the table to grab her flailing arms, knocking it over in the process. More screaming and shrieking enveloped the room.

"*You do remember me. You do remember me. You do remember me. You do remember me. You do remember me. You do remember me.*"

And as soon as it had began it was over. She ran out of the café, turning right; up St. Peter's Street towards Essex Road. I pulled some money from my pocket, I have no idea how much, but it was more than enough to cover what we had ordered. I left it on the table and I ran out after her, leaving the man and the woman from the whitewashed office block and the bored woman behind the counter to clear up the mess. I ran after her. I could see her, running erratically, people stopping to watch, to ask her if she was okay, as she made her way, clumsily up towards the busy Essex Road. I shouted after her. She continued to run away, heading for wherever it was she was heading. All I could do was follow her, up towards the Essex Road. As I drew nearer I could hear her sobs. When she stopped at the top of St. Peter's Street with the junction of Essex Road she looked frantically from her left to her right, over and over again. Essex Road was, as usual, unbelievably busy, and she was clearly unsure of which way to go. I shouted to her. Passers-by in the street turned to look; cyclists and people in parked cars, people sitting outside cafés. As I finally got to her I reached out to put my hand on her shoulder. She turned to face me, screaming as if I was trying to attack her. I immediately let go of her and she wriggled free and, without looking, ran straight into the road. The number 38 bus screeched to a shuddering halt, throwing many of its crammed-in passengers, who were standing by the doors and in the aisles, to the floor. I could hear screams and much shouting. The bus was inches from her. The whole of Essex Road had stopped doing whatever it was it was doing and everything was focussed on her, standing in the middle of the road, facing the number 38 bus. She began to laugh, running to the other side of the road. I stayed opposite her and began to walk. I acted like I wasn't with her, like I was a spectator, but everyone within the vicinity knew that we were together. I followed her once more as she continued to run, this time with quickening, assured footfalls, with purpose and determination. When I had walked far enough away from the initial scene in the road I too began to run. I ran as quickly as my legs and body could carry me, after her, on the opposite side of Essex Road to her. Heading up towards Balls Pond Road.

It was a Saturday morning. I must have been in my early twenties. I was with an old companion whom I have since lost touch with. She was older than me and was taking me to a new shop in Soho she wanted to visit that sold expensive, designer underwear. We boarded the bus on Balls Pond Road. As soon as I stepped on board I knew something was wrong. The driver was glaring at me. He held out his hand suddenly, beckoning me to stop. I waited, thinking that a young mother, or an elderly lady needed to get on the bus before me. I turned around: four regular-looking passengers were waiting there, the driver asked them on board before me with nothing, as far as I could see, that suggested they should each receive preferential treatment over me. My friend was waiting for me upstairs. I waited patiently until the four ordinary passengers had paid their fare.

"Excuse me . . ."

"Yes?"

"Why did you just halt me to let other people on before me?"

"You know why?"

"*Pardon*?"

"I said . . . you know why."

"What do you mean?"

"*I said you know why*?"

"What!"

"Last night . . ."

"*Last night*?"

"Yes."

"*What?!*"

"I remember you from last night . . . You were on my bus . . ."

"Last night? I wasn't*!*"

"Yes, you were*!*"

"*I wasn't* . . . I didn't even get a bus last night."

"Don't fuck around with me! I'm calling the police. It was you who spat at me. *Last night*, as you were all leaving, after I asked you all to leave my bus for harassing passengers . . ."

"Look here, I have no idea whatsoever what it is you are talking about. I didn't get on a bus last night."

"Don't fuck with me. I'm phoning the police . . ."

"I'm not fucking with you, *I'm telling the truth* . . ."

"I'm phoning the police."

"Why!? Why!? Why!? What have I done? I just want to get on your bus!"

"*Right*. I'm radioing the depot right now . . . H-H-H-Hello . . . Y-Y-Yes, Okay, I need the police, I am the driver of . . ."

The driver proceeded to inform the depot of his exact whereabouts the previous night when the alleged incident, supposedly involving me, took place. He described me to the person on the other end of the line. I realised that he could have been trying to frighten me, though, as some act of revenge or something. After the phone call he turned back to me. People started to grumble and complain. His face grew redder with each second that passed us by.

"Listen, here, *get off my fucking bus!* If you get off my bus now the police won't arrest you. *Get off my fucking bus . . .*"

I realised his call to the depot had indeed been faked.

"*No*. It's my right as an innocent person to remain on this bus . . ."

"If you don't get off my bus this instant I will turn off the engine and no one will go anywhere . . ."

"Turn it off . . . I'm going nowhere."

He turned off the engine.

The entire bus became silent.

Then, when the passengers had finally realised what was happening, everything seemed to erupt: a cacophony of anger and hatred. All it took was the silence; the sense that things had stalled.

The passengers' shrill voices cut into me.

"*Get off!*"

"*Get off the bus, you fool!*"

"*Get off! I need to be somewhere!*"

"*Now!*"

"*Leave, fuckin' innit!*"

"*I'll throw you off if you don't move!*"

"*Get off now!*"

As all this was happening, the driver stepped out of his cabin. He was small and stocky with a low centre of gravity. He gripped me by the collar, and in one swift move managed to open the emergency exit and throw me off the bus and onto the pavement. I noticed my friend, halfway up the stairs to the upper deck, looking down at me. Before my friend could get off the bus the driver shut the door, started up the engine and resumed his journey. I can still remember each face, peering down through the window as the bus trundled away from me, bathing me in its rotten fumes.

It was at that moment, there on the cold pavement, that I realised I was ordinary and not destined for great things.

- ten -

We were at the top end of Essex Road, near to Balls Pond Road. She suddenly turned right, heading east into De Beauvoir Town. The traffic was noisy, that incessant London drone. Gaggles of scooterists were hogging the road, reviving their hairdryer-like engines at the lights, cutting corners and generally terrifying any pedestrians who attempted to cross the road before them. Some took particular delight in inching forwards, as if attempting to mow one down, as people crossed at the pelican crossing. The road seemed to be filled with them, buzzing about like swarms of angry wasps without a care in the world. It was completely depressing.

I've never wanted to hang around in packs. Even when I was at the age I was supposed to, and my friends ventured off to Highbury to watch the Arsenal every other weekend, I would make my excuses until they eventually stopped asking me.

She had stopped running and was walking along quite slowly now, naturally puffed and out of breath. She stopped a couple of times to stroke a cat that had been following her; a small tabby cat that looked undernourished, though probably wasn't—being as most domesticated cats are overfed and quite fat. She crouched close to it, down to the ground, the cat looking up, circling her, rubbing its scent glands against her shins, lifting up its tail, exposing its anus for her to sniff, to inspect, to classify DNA, then falling to the ground, rolling onto its back in complete and utter submission.

I stopped walking and rested by a garden wall to watch. She obviously knew I was there, watching her and the cat, but she didn't once acknowledge my presence behind her.

The cat soon trotted away, content with itself, as an Islington Refuge Collection van pulled into the street, its pack of binmen it contained quickly scurrying in and out of gardens, rummaging around for black sacks of rubbish. The cat fled quickly, down into a basement flat's front garden—if you could call it that—and out of the way.

Again, she began to walk, although she set off with a little bit more purpose this time. It seemed she had finally decided where it was she wanted to go. I naturally presumed she was going home, back to the safety of her flat, but she turned immediately right onto Southgate Road, heading in the direction of the canal again. It made perfect sense to me: she had to find somewhere she could feel anonymous, where she could observe and become invisible—where she could belong. I followed her along Southgate Road, past the Northgate Pub and the small cluster of shops next to it. The canal wasn't that far away.

- eleven -

I was beginning to realise that I had lost control—what little of it I had had in the first place, that is. No—that I had never *had* control. Boredom had left me behind, I had succumb to its weight, its unheard-of centre within me. I had embraced it and it had completely consumed me and now I was bored of it. I was bored of boredom. There was nothing

I could really do about this. I was like everyone else: I
needed something to fill the gap, the time that dragged us,
and it, along with it, to return me to the ground beneath
my feet and hide away from our gaping hole like everyone
else. Who was she to me? Why was she suddenly in my life?
Was she there to serve as some warning? Revealing all to
me? Everything that isn't really there?

- twelve -

Following her along Southgate Road, as I did, seemed real
to me, like I was snapping back from a daydream, or some
unknowable space outside of myself. As we neared the canal
things began to focus within me again; things became normal as we drew near to its space—the only space we could
exist together within, where things started, at the boundary
of Hackney on Islington, on the canal, by the side of the
rusting iron bridge that connected everything.

I was standing by the site of the old Thomas Briggs factory, near where the old gates still stood, the last remnants
of the old bell still visible, *Factory* carved, imperiously into
the gnarled masonry beneath it. On the many times I would
pass it by I would always make a point of touching it, press-
ing into it, where the button for the bell used to be (which
had long since gone), trying to imagine the factory workers queuing outside each morning, or streaming through
the open gates of an evening after a hard shift with the
machines and the clatter, and the toil. The area where the
old factory stood is called Rosemary Gardens, and nearby
stood two pubs—one now converted into a house—where
there used to be cockfighting and, much later, trips in an
air balloon that used to be tethered there. It's also the site
were the Levellers were first formed: the radical left-wing

movement of the seventeenth century whose members wore a sprig of rosemary in their hats at their meetings, held in an old alehouse that once stood on that site. The remaining pub—The Rosemary Branch—is named in honour of them. The whole area, a nondescript place to most people, holds huge historical significance. Yet people will merrily walk by it without a care in the world. Upstairs in the Rosemary Branch is a small theatre. One evening I got to talking to a young actress at the bar. She was starring in some production there. I remember her staring out of the window and seriously ask me: *'How does one get anywhere from here? We're in the middle of nowhere.'* I wanted to explain to her everything I knew about Rosemary Gardens. I wanted to say to her that things didn't revolve around her, that things had already happened many times over in that very spot. But I didn't. I sipped my drink and listened to her ignorant nonsense.

I could smell the murky water of the canal emanating up onto the road where it ran parallel with the canal for two-hundred yards or so before stopping—Southgate Road, that is—at New North Road, the canal carrying on down towards Islington.

She stopped. She was standing by the Rosemary Branch.

The murky water took on a different stench up there by the road, less pungent, less silty. It had mixed with the exhaust fumes and transformed into something else, machine-like, industrious, something old tainted by a new age.

She was looking out over the canal, her back turned to the Rosemary Branch, out towards Hoxton and the City, farther out towards the Swiss Re building, Tower 42, and the newer skeletal structures in progress appearing here and there—newer buildings about to tower over the London skyline en masse, continuing its progress, an unremitting vista of cranes and building sites, scaffolding and pollution, sprawled in all its vulgarity, ugliness, and beauty before her.

I stopped and waited for her to walk across the road and take the steps down to the canal. She seemed to be frozen, as if every atom within her had stopped sparking. The traffic trundled by in both directions between us, a line of cars in one direction, some cyclists and a number 76 bus in the other. Behind her, to her left, stood the old Gainsborough Studios where Hitchcock had made a few of his films. The whole building was now expensive flats, though in the courtyard lies an impressive sculpture of him in honour. I raised my eyes up above her and looked at the top row of flats. In the end flat, over-looking the canal, I could see a man and a woman standing on their balcony,. They were facing each other, both, it seemed, wearing white bath robes. The woman was gesticulating frantically; the man was quite passive. They were both completely unaware that they could be seen. The man held his head to his hands after a short while and then lurched forwards, placing each hand on her shoulders, hoping to calm her down it seemed, but this action only served to enrage her further. She stepped back and ran into the flat, out of view. She was screaming at him, I could catch it briefly during the short breaks in the traffic. Then she ran back out onto the balcony; she was still screaming and gesticulating wildly. The man had now sat down at the table and chairs they had up there, so all I could see was her: her arms, windmill-like, flailing, forming a circular mass around her body. Then she stopped. She pointed towards him and stopped screaming. He suddenly rose to his feet, becoming visible to me again. He stepped towards her and attempted to embrace her again. She pulled away, back into their expensive flat, leaving him there. He leant over the balcony, resting on his elbows, his head in his hands again, staring down to the canal below.

When I looked back she had gone. At first I panicked, my heart skipping a number of beats. I swallowed my breath and looked for her about the road frantically. Then it hit me again: she was going back there to see him, to watch him. She was going back to the canal, like I always knew she would.

I've often thought that we seek reality in places and not in ourselves. These places can be anywhere we like them to be: a desert island, the beach, a nightclub, in the arms of a lover in a far-off land, rock climbing, up in the clouds, down in the depths of the deepest ocean, in space—ultimately in space. These places, this space, can be anything we want it to be. We need things, extra things that help us to make sense of it all; we need the space where things can happen, where these spaces can become a thing—it is only at that point, when space becomes a *thing* to us, that we truly feel real.

The thing is: I don't feel real, and yet the space had become a *thing* to me—to us, I'd thought. That space that we had shared together, by the canal, the whitewashed office block, the rusting iron bridge and the coots, the Canada geese, and the swans . . . It all seemed such a long time ago now. Such a long time.

- thirteen -

I walked down the steps and onto the towpath. I could see her up ahead, walking towards the bridge in the distance. She was walking quite slowly, but still with some kind of purpose. In the canal, to her immediate left, following alongside her were three or four coots; they were after food, thinking she had come to feed them. Up ahead, towards the bridge and the whitewashed office block, beyond that space, I could see the two swans resting by the far bank.

I honestly had no idea what I was going to say to her; I just knew that I was going to confront her, to ask her if anything she had told me was the truth. I wanted her to look me in the eye and simply tell me the truth. And then, once she had—and I hoped that she would—I would simply walk away and out of her life forever.

Memories are strange things; I don't particularly understand them. I don't understand why they appear, or where they return to. Memories were once real things, but I don't understand what they are now. Still, it seems now they are all I have. All I have to fall back on, like a series of photographs.

I remember my mother saying something to me when I was a small child. I had been angry over the death of my grandmother. My mother comforted me after the funeral, in a small room at the back of my grandmother's old house in Whitechapel. She said to me that nobody dies, because the deceased remain in the memory of the living. She said that that was all I had to think of whenever I became confused. I wanted to say to her then, right there in that small back room in Whitechapel, that even the living have to die—and that memories have to die with them. I wanted to tell her that nobody lives on forever. Well, they can't. Of course, I never got around to saying this. I controlled my anger and returned to the large room where my family were seated on odd chairs, eating, drinking, and continuing this belief.

And now? All I have are my memories of this. And soon they will disappear with me, too.

- fourteen -

I could feel the wind on my face. The murky water was choppy. I could see the dark clouds gathering for more rain above me, forming as if they had been purposely pushed there, the whole world a fiction. Above me, above her. The first droplets of the downpour—the greasy drizzle burgeoning into heavy globules—hit me as I returned my gaze to her, sheltering under the rusting iron bridge. It was a complete deluge. The rain bounced up from the towpath, back up into the atmosphere, back up my legs and trousers as I quickened my pace towards the bridge. Towards her.

She eventually looked up at me as I finally approached. She looked mawkish, and like she was sweating, but it was probably the rain. She was obviously embarrassed with herself. We stood next to each other without speaking. I listened to the rain. It was making a thunderous racket.

I felt like I was in a tent during a storm. I had always loved that feeling: the warmth and security of the waterproof canvas. I had always loved the sound of each individual droplet of water hitting the roof of the tent, one after the other, all at the same time, a cacophony of mini-aquatic explosions. I had always felt safe underneath the canvas when we camped in back gardens as children. I had always hoped for rain: nothing could touch me when it rained. The rain bounced off the surface of the canal. She was leaning against the darkened brick, her whole frame hunched like she was in pain, or bored, waiting for something to happen.

It was as if all that had taken place—all our conversations, all my following her and worrying—had never taken place at all, no matter how real her grimace looked. That moment, underneath the rusting iron bridge, laid itself out before me, almost as if it was the first time I had ever set eyes upon her. The rain had kept the towpath empty, even the cyclists and dog-walkers had been driven back home. It seemed to be the perfect space for us. A perfect time.

I said the words without looking at her, concentrating on a clump of earth and detritus that formed a coot's nest on the far bank of the canal towards a barge that was moored to the left of the rusting iron bridge.

"Are you real?"

"Pardon?"

"*Are you real?*"

"Yes. Of course I'm *real*."

"Are you really here? In this space with me?"

"*Of course I'm here* . . . You're speaking to me, right?"

"Right."

"Well?"

"Well, *what*?"

"Then, I am real. Just like everything I have told you is real. Just like all of this is real . . . The canal, the bridge that connects everything, shelters us . . . the swan over there . . . Unfortunately, it's all real, yes. Every minute particle of it . . ."

"What do you mean?"

"Unfortunately, for us—for all of us—it's all real."

"Well, what was all that about?"

"*In the café?*"

"Yes. In the café."

"The usual things . . ."

"Well . . . ?"

"Finding our little foothold in the void . . ."

"The *void*?"

"Yes."

"I don't understand . . ."

"*Love . . . happiness . . . understanding* . . . All the clichés that torment us, that are supposed to torment us, that we are told to be tormented by . . . Everything that leads to this . . ."

"To what, exactly?"

"This. *Here*. Underneath the bridge . . ."

"What do you mean?"

"Everything leads to here . . ."

"Where?"

"The bridge."

"Listen, I really don't understand, I really don't . . ."

"This is our moment . . . everything has found its location . . ."

"Because of the bridge?"

"*Yes.*"

I didn't really understand what she was talking about. It clearly meant something to her, so I made it look like it meant something to me: I paused, I rubbed my chin thoughtfully, my right leg began to shake; I nodded my head a couple of times at moments when I thought it felt I should. She looked at me. I could feel her gaze, her eyes burning into me. I refused to look at her. I concentrated on the coots' nest ahead, beyond the bridge, next to the moored barge. I refused to acknowledge her, and although I had no idea why, it still felt truly glorious.

And then she looked away.

The underside of the bridge was covered in years of grime and weathered decay. Streams of rust-coloured water poured down the brickwork of the wall behind us, covering a lifetime of graffiti and scratches and marks left behind from those who had passed under and sought refuge before us. All those before us, who had had their own moments there, too. All those moments that had been acted out beneath the bridge. It was right, somehow, no matter how much I couldn't understand it.

On the canal, before the offices were offices, when they were derelict warehouses, debris from another age, when Wenlock Basin was empty of barges and swans, my brother taught me to climb a tree just up from the rusting iron bridge. It's still there, nestled and towering, by the new wall. Even back then it was a tall, imposing tree, perfect for climbing. All my friends had climbed it; all of them could reach the highest branches, to sit upon and watch the comings and goings of the canal below. I used to stand by the trunk, contemplating how I could get up there with them. I knew I couldn't do it though. I remember the day my brother taught me to climb the tree. I followed him up, copying each of his movements, placing my hands and feet exactly where he just had, carefully, to the millimetre, slowly, from one thick branch up to the next. He showed me how to rest the weight of my whole body on one foot in order to spring up to the next, whilst reaching upwards with a hand, transferring the weight on my foot into my arm, into my grip on the next branch. He told me that I could never fall. He told me, over and over, that it was impossible to fall. I followed him to the very top of the tree without looking down, knowing that if I did it would be over for me. I followed him to where the thinner and younger branches swayed, under our combined weight, where it was possible to feel the gentle sway, the movement of the whole tree. We rested there. Hanging on tightly. He finally told me to look back down, to see how high we had climbed, but I couldn't. I could only concentrate on the rooftops in the distance. I couldn't look down to where we had climbed from, because to me the height was monstrous. I could see over most of the maisonettes in the Packington Estate out to the northeast and over towards Canonbury. My brother was asking me, over and over, to look down, to see how high we were. I knew at that moment that I should never have climbed the tree with him, and that I shouldn't look back down, but for some reason I did. I looked back down, to the ground, from where we had started, and as soon as our height actually registered fully within me I closed my eyes tightly, unable to open them again, and I screamed. I screamed at my brother to help me down from the tree. He told me to open my eyes, so that I could follow him back down. I could feel him begin his descent, slowly, assuredly, asking me all the while to open my eyes and follow him, but I couldn't. He pleaded with me, but each gentle sway of the branch I was clinging to forced me to clench my eyes tighter together and grip the branch all the more securely. I shouted for him not to leave me, to get back up to the top of the tree with me, but I could feel him moving away from me, back down the tree towards the ground. Finally, he stood at the bottom of the tree, shouting to me to open my eyes. He shouted and shouted for me to trust him, that he would be there for each of my steps back down, that I could do it and there was nothing to be afraid of. He shouted up to me that he was one hundred percent confident that I could actually do it. I opened my eyes, the bright daylight pouring into them. I looked down and soon he began to come into focus. He looked so tiny down there on the ground. He looked so small, like an insect I could crush with my fingers, hold in the cup of my palm or place inside a matchbox. It felt like I could step on him with the heel of my shoe. I looked down at him, he stretched out his arms, assuring me that he would catch me if I slipped. I finally began my descent. He talked me all the way through it: which branches to hold on to, where to place my foot next, et cetera. With each step he became larger, until I hit the ground and he towered over me again, and he picked me up and carried me, up on his shoulders, all the way back home.

We have never really spoken about the day he taught me to climb that tree. I have always wanted to thank him. I have always wanted to tell him that day mattered to me.

- fifteen -

The rain became quite unbelievable. A continuous sheet of water poured down incessantly from the dark, grey clouds above. It was as if the dredgers had planned it, to help clean up anything that they had left behind. But I didn't want things to be washed away. I wanted things to remain the same. No, I wanted things to begin anew, as if it was my first day on the canal again, my first venture towards it. She could never have realised that this was how I actually felt at that precise moment—and if she did, I know now that she wouldn't have given it much thought. I often wonder, if she had the chance, if she would have thought about it enough to have done something about our pointless situation? Maybe she would have turned herself in to the police? Or told me that everything was a complete figment of her own imagination?

I peered from under the bridge. The heavy, cold, droplets of rain hit my cheeks, soaking my face and neck. Most of the windows in the whitewashed office block had steamed up, but the windows that protected the private offices of the office elite—i.e., middle management and above—remained clear and intact from condensation. She was staring into the murky water, watching the rain bounce back up from it. Pretty soon droplets of rusty, dirty water began to fall from the underside of the bridge to pool at my feet. I noticed that the towpath had been stained by it, where each droplet connected back to the ground. Every time the clouds above burst, the brown stain—achieved over years' worth of downpours—came to resemble the rings of a newly cut tree trunk.

I was sitting on the cold, linoleum floor, looking up towards the hole where the water was pouring in. I was mesmerised by it. I realised that things weren't as they seemed, that things could happen and change. I realised that things could suddenly begin that you never thought imaginable. I could be imparting wisdom from the present onto the past, as this is how I see things now, I'm not sure; I do know that it seemed absurd to me that instead of fixing the hole my mother and father placed a large cooking pot directly underneath the leak, collecting the water and then pouring it away, down the sink, when the pot was nearly full. They seemed content with this repetitive activity, as if the hole didn't matter to them (even though it must have mattered to them, as the leak was eventually fixed). They didn't seem too fussed. In fact, they found the whole scenario quite amusing, my father especially, laughing as my mother rushed into the kitchen every now and again, breaking from her crossword puzzle, to empty the near-full cooking pot. I was sitting by the pot, watching the long stream of water pour through the hole and down, in one constant stream, into it. I loved the sound it made, the perpetual trickle that, at that time to me, seemed infinite. That sound still penetrates my memory.

The leak fascinated me because I couldn't fathom where it was coming from. I knew it came through the hole, but beyond that I was empty of ideas and understanding, although I knew it had to come from somewhere. I couldn't understand why all that water would appear from a little hole in the ceiling of my parents' kitchen. A hole, a crack, a fissure in the ceiling, it seemed to me as if I was witness-ing some form of magic: that something was pulling all that water down from the sky above, down through our ceiling, towards me, so I could delight in the sound it made. And then I realised there was no room above the kitchen, the kitchen was an extension attached onto the house after it had been originally built. There must have been a hole in the roof, and the water was being pulled down from the clouds above. It was rainwater being pulled back down to earth, through our roof, into our small kitchen. This revelation thrilled me.

Where did all that water go to? When my mother poured it down the sink, down all those pipes, down again through the subterranean sewage and water networks beneath our feet. I understood enough to realise that it didn't disappear. I wanted to know exactly where it was going, where it would end up next, the water from my ceiling. Surely it all had to end up somewhere? Surely it still can't be continuing its journey away from me? Surely it must have come to some sort of stop? Settled, in some form or other, somewhere? But why should these thoughts, these little, annoying thoughts matter to me? Surely I should let them wash over me? I truly feel they are of no use to me now. No use at all. Yet, they persist, pouring into me.

She was squinting. It looked like she was trying to focus on something that wasn't there, something invisible down by her feet. She began to kick her shoes into some loose gravel.

"We could have seen all this coming, you know . . ."

"What do you mean?"

"Well, it's all so obvious, isn't it?"

"*Is it*? What is?"

"This is . . ."

She looked up. She began a long, drawn out yawn, scratching her left cheek at the same time. When she had finished the yawn, which seemed to last far longer than necessary, she looked at me, through me, nowhere in particular, before she continued.

"It's all over."

"What is?"

"This is . . ."

"What do you mean by *this*?"

She shrugged her shoulders, child-like and unconcerned, but I knew she shrugged not out of ignorance, but out of some desire for me to understand. It was better for her not to say anything, or not too much, in the hope that she could continue. Eventually, after taking some time to bite her nails, she began to talk, this time with a little bit more clarity.

"He's married, you know."

"Who is?"

"*Him* . . . Him, across there, in that office block, that stinking office . . . He's married. But not to her, not to that woman, his *colleague* from the café. No, he's married to someone else."

"Oh. *Him*."

"Yes. *Him*. He has children too, two daughters. I've seen him with them. I know where they live. I know what she, *his wife*, does. I know everything there is to know about them . . . With their perfect life that isn't perfect, him acting like it's the most natural thing in the world, you know, that's how bad he is, a walking male cliché. He acts like he's doing nothing wrong. He swans around that stinking office in his expensive clothes that are a little too tight for comfort, he swans around that stinking office without a care in the world. But I know who he is. I could change all that. I could change all of it. He doesn't even remember me . . . We have already met, we have spoken to each other before today, you know . . ."

"Where? When did you speak?"

"We have spoken before, briefly. He placed his hand on my shoulder . . . He tried to comfort me."

"*When? Where?*"

"Yet . . . that moment, the moment we shared, he has no recollection of it now . . . He doesn't want to remember, he has blotted me out of his life . . . He chooses to ignore who I am, *what I did* . . . What I did to change things in his life . . ."

"*What!?*"

"When I chose to kill his father. When I took his father from him . . . Has it taken you this long to work it out? A cliché as grand as this?"

"Where did you speak to him, his son?"

"At his father's funeral."

"*You went to the funeral?*"

"Yes."

"*Why on earth would you do that?*"

"I sat on the back row in the church, near Old Street. On my own. Looking at the coffin, with him inside, all alone. The family mourning his death, openly, repeating the patterns and action of the mourners they had observed before them as children. I could see him, the son, ahead, sitting up at the front, next to his wife. During the ceremony, I think it was Catholic, he turned around to look at me three times. I knew that he had noticed me . . . He must have been wondering why I was there . . . A friend of his father's maybe? A friend of his mother's? But that didn't make sense to him. I'm too young, too different from them . . . Maybe he thought I was someone connected with the church? You get that don't you?"

"Get what?"

"Lone women, with no direction, who dedicate their whole lives to subservience in the church . . ."

"But you said you both have spoken to each other . . . That he touched your shoulder?"

"We did . . ."

"Why did you do that?"

"I wanted to tell him that I was sorry . . ."

"*Sorry?*"

"Yes. Sorry."

"So . . . he knows . . . ?"

"*Knows?*"

"That you killed his father?"

"No. He was too stupid, thinking of himself too much to realise just what I meant. When I think back about it now it must have happened too suddenly for him to have realised, let alone to remember later on. But when I think back . . . to that moment . . . It was the longest moment in my entire life. My only moment. The only moment that mattered if I think about it. To say sorry . . . To admit . . . So, I was standing outside when he approached me. I was watching all the mourners as they stepped out of the church after me. There were quite a few. I just wanted to watch them. I didn't want to speak to anyone. I wanted to quietly leave when I had finished, you know? When I had had enough. But then he just walked over to me. He just smiled and asked me if we knew each other. I told him that I knew his father. His smile broadened. I looked at him and after a short intake of breath I just let the words tumble from my mouth: '*I'm sorry, for what happened. I'm sorry your father had to die.*' It was at this moment that he put his hand on my shoulder. It felt right, *so* right. But he didn't even give me a second thought, couldn't even remember me, so, so it's all over isn't it? It's all come to nothing . . . Everything is just moving along as it always does, in steadfast indifference . . . Nothing we do matters, nothing I could ever say matters. I killed him and it doesn't matter."

"How could he recognise you . . . ? In the café . . . Funerals are stressful times."

"He *had* to recognise me. That's all he had to do . . ."

"But . . . Well, at least . . . at least you got to say sorry to him."

"It means nothing if it's never heard, absolutely nothing."

I shuffled closer to her. I was happy that we had found shelter beneath the engineered hulk of the bridge.

It was my grandfather's funeral. I was standing around the open grave as his dark coffin was lowered into the sodden, muddy hole. I was standing with my father and mother. She was crying, my father stoically staring at the coffin, his father inside. We sheltered from the rain under my father's large umbrella. My brother was facing me, on the other side of the open grave, standing with an aunt. I remember the sound of the rain hitting the muddy earth, the gravestones, the scattered sarcophagi and the umbrellas of the collected mourners present, drowning out the pious words of the vicar. I couldn't hear a word he was saying, although I knew he was saying something as I could see his mouth moving, forming words. I could see him gesticulating above the coffin. But I couldn't hear anything. It was useless. It became meaningless. It didn't seem real, something that was supposed to be the only thing in life that was real and meant something, but it just didn't seem real at all. Everyone seemed to be acting out their parts, in the mud and the rain. None of this seemed to bother those present, as if they had heard it all before anyway, accepting it all, as if that was how it should be. I looked up at a relative whom I barely knew. She was loudly sobbing. There was something odd about her tears and sobs, something not quite right, as if she was really thinking of something else, pretending to listen and care, her mind elsewhere, hoping it would all soon be over, so she could get back to her car and out of the rain. I looked at everyone else. It was obvious that they didn't really want to be there. It was obvious to me that they had simply been told to act that way.

* * *

The rain was horrendous. It was pouring towards the earth like the soil demanded it. I wanted it to stop, as much as I knew how futile my wishes were. The clouds were darkening further, and the whole canal—especially looking out from underneath the bridge—began to take on an altogether threatening hue: dark, angry and metallic, like it was primed with violent electricity. Threatening. The once murky water looked jet black, like a river of oil. She blew her nose on a handkerchief and brushed her hair back behind her ears.

"I don't mind the rain . . ."

"It rains too much for me to like it . . ."

"All I wanted was for him to recognise me . . ."

"But . . . why?"

"So he can see I'm just like everyone else, that I'm not some monster. So he could see that I was just like him . . . before . . ."

"Before what?"

"Before the police eventually find me and I'm not given the chance to make people realise that I'm just like them . . ."

As she was saying these things to me I was aware of some movement above us. At first it was hard to distinguish it from the noise of the rain hitting the bridge and the water, but it soon became apparent to me that there were people up on the bridge. At first I presumed it to be people, office workers or locals maybe, passing over the canal on errands or something, but the voices—there were more than one— weren't moving. The voices remained directly above us. I then realised that the voices weren't adult voices, they were too energetic, too excitable. I knew that it was them. I knew that it was the Pack Crew. I just knew it was them. I tried to peek out above the bridge, but it was impossible to see anything. I imagined the redheaded lad to be there, he must have been there, fiddling with his mobile phone, or lighter, spitting indiscriminately onto the tarmac at his feet. I imagined their hoods up, shielding their faces from the sheets of rain. I wondered what it was they could be doing up there, above us, on the bridge in the pouring rain. I knew they had to be up to something: no one in their right minds, even a teenage gang, would stand on a bridge, over a murky canal, exposed to the torrential downpour, for the sake of it, to merely hang out. Nobody does that. I knew that they must be doing something nefarious, that they were standing on that bridge for a particular reason. I signalled to her, gesticulating to her to look up and listen. She did what I said, understanding my signals and listened for a short while, then she shrugged her shoulders. I put my finger to my lips; I didn't want us to be heard; I didn't want them to know we were just below them.

The first time I ran away from home—after some trivial argument with my brother about football or something—I ran all the way to the canal, eastwards, towards Broadway Market. By a bridge, I found some scrubland that was bordered by a red brick wall at one end. The wall was quite old. It had probably stood there for over one hundred years or more before I finally reached it that day. It stood at the farthest end from the canal. Behind it was a derelict print works that was being used as a scrap yard. I ran through the long grass towards the wall and sat there beneath it with the moss and the damp, breathing heavily, determined never to go back home, before I spotted the old front door that had been dumped there in the long grass. It was still quite solid, having apparently not been exposed for that long to the elements, so I lifted it up and leant the door horizontally against the decaying red brickwork. I thought nothing of disturbing the newly-formed ecosystem in the process and relished my new impromptu den. I climbed inside. It soon began to rain; I was completely protected from the elements. I felt warm; safe. I must have fallen asleep, because I awoke to voices: two men on the other side of the wall. I can remember what the two men were talking about: they were talking about a woman. I presumed she was the wife, or girlfriend of one of the men.

Man A: She just took off.

Man B: When?

Man A: Last night. With him.

Man B: Why?

Man A: Said she was fucking bored.

Man B:: *Bored*?

Man A: Yeah. *Fucking bored*.

Man B: With what?

Man A: With me!

Man B: With you?

Man A: Yeah. *With me*.

Man B: *Fuck*. That's shit.

Man A: I know. I want to fucking *kill* her.

I wet myself, I think. I was terrified. My damp trousers biting into my shivering thighs, my skin reacting, tightening, feeding my burgeoning paroxysms of fear. I closed my eyes until they both walked away. Whoever they were, however normal they were, or psychopathic, I didn't want to see them, or them to see me. It was the wall that saved me from them. It was the decaying, one-hundred-year-old, red brick wall that separated me from them. It no longer exists.

That night I walked home in the dark. I walked into my parents' house, trying to act as if everything was okay. I was happy when my parents' combined anger subsided into waves of relief and comfort. After my father had lectured me my mother took me aside. We walked into the kitchen, away from my father and my brother—who seemed to have found the whole episode highly amusing—and the rest of the house. We stood by the kitchen sink, it was still full of unwashed dishes. My mother began to wash a plate under a tap. She didn't say that much, and most of it I find difficult to remember, but I do remember one thing, and it has left a mark in me, she said: *"There's no point in running away. Never run away, all you find is yourself. There's nothing else to find."* I didn't understand her then, all those years ago, and it's hard for me to understand those words even now— but I think I might. I think she might have meant no matter where we hide, no matter into which hole we choose to burrow, we have to make room for the shadow that always accompanies us—wherever it is we go—revealing to us our true nature: the sheer, undeniable weight of it all. The beauty of it being this: weight isn't distinguishable by some thing. There is no *thing*. It is weight, the paradox being that it—the weight that envelops us—somehow calms us.

At least I think that's what she meant. I should have listened to my mother.

- sixteen -

The voices above us on the rusting iron bridge became louder, more excitable and energetic. Something was happening up there. They were doing something. At first, they presented themselves, the collective voices, as a continuing, muffled voice, a collective voice that could not be understood, a rising noise of undecipherable syllables and accents, a slight rumpus of varying octaves. Yet, the more intently I listened, each voice began to separate itself from the other, the once homogenous mass of amusement began to filter through, as if I had finally cracked some form of verbal cipher, and I began to pick out and select certain words, each too arbitrary to fit into any context.

"_____There_____"
"_____Now_____"
"_____Again____"
"__Let_____"
"_____No_"
"_____Aim_____"
"_____Up_____"
"____Do_____"
"_____Missed_____"

It was difficult to understand what was happening up above us. I imagined the redheaded youth to be orchestrating the whole thing—he was leading whatever it was they were doing up there. I wanted them to go away, to leave me alone. I wanted to expel them from my life, or for them to become bored with whatever it was they were doing and walk elsewhere and do something else in the rain, away from me, away from the canal—away from us. But something was occupying them, something had rooted them to that spot above us, something exciting, something that passed the time for them. Whatever it was they were doing.

Their voices began to filter down below the bridge, reverberating between us, within its shelter. I began to detect the beginnings of short, vigorous sentences, followed by little bursts of verbalised anticipation.

"_____There! It's there!_____"
"____Do it now, again!_____"
"____You missed!_____"
"_Up a bit! There! Again, do it again!_____"
"_____Let me have a go!_____"
"_____Just hit it!_____"
"_____Come on! Give me a go!_____"
"____No. It's my turn!_____"
"_____I'll get the fucker!____ _____"
"_____I'll get it!_____"

"_____Shoot it! There! Shoot it!_____"
"_____You're wasting shots!_____"
"_____Give it here!_____"

At first, it sounded like someone being slapped on the back quite playfully. Then it happened again. And then again.

The fourth time that it happened I noticed something dart down into the murky water by my right. At first I thought it was some sort of bird, but it wasn't. It had travelled at an incredible speed, as when I turned to look where it had entered the canal there was no sign of it. I scanned the water's surface for any other signs. It seemed as if whatever it was must have entered quite close to the two swans, who were sheltering on the other bank from the rain. As this was happening, the sound of a low-flying helicopter suddenly rumbled, somewhere above, the sound of its rotor blades cutting through the dismal, rain-soaked atmosphere. The sound was quite deafening. It must have been the ambulance service cutting across the city to some accident. It definitely wasn't the police helicopter as that could be detected by a slower, deeper sound. As loud as the helicopter was above me I was still unable to detect where it was heading to. It soon passed us by. Then, all I could hear was the rain again. I checked the swans: they seemed quite unperturbed, as if nothing was really happening. Their mechanisms and cognitive motors had obviously retired for the afternoon. Then, as I was thinking this, another thing darted into the water at a ferocious speed and angle. This time the big male swan inched nearer to the bank, noticing too that something odd, and possibly dangerous, had happened. Then, all of the voices became unbearably clear.

"Come on! You can do better than that, man!"
"That was fucking close, innit!"
"I can hit it! I can hit it!"

"Give the thing to me, innit!"

I turned back to her, putting my right index finger to my lips. She narrowed her eyes at me, a little nonplussed if anything. I pointed up to the bridge and then over to the swans. She yawned and looked at her wristwatch for what seemed like the umpteenth time; eventually she shrugged her shoulders again. This time I began to point more vigorously at the two swans, but still she seemed lost in a world of her own thinking. I walked up to her and whispered in her ear.

"They're trying to shoot the swans . . ."

At first she ignored me, but then she suddenly turned to look at the swans: nothing was happening, the same rain pouring down, around them into the now quite choppy, murky water. She turned to me, her eyes widening, and stared as if to ask me what the hell I was implying. As she did this I saw over her shoulder another thing dart into the water and this time, for reasons beyond my comprehension, I could actually see what it was, as if I had suddenly possessed the power to slow things down, following its full trajectory into the canal, inches to the left of the male swan: it was an arrow, a short, stubby arrow, like the kind used for crossbows. They, the four youths who had attacked me— The Pack Crew—were shooting arrows at the two swans. They were shooting the swans! I charged out onto the sodden towpath and looked up at the bridge—all I could see was the dark metallic crossbow, resting on the iron railing, aimed downwards, diagonally across the canal towards the swans.

"Now! Pull the fucking trigger, man, innit!"

That was all I heard. I followed the arrow down as it shot towards the large male cob, followed its forty-five degree trajectory down, its sharp point heading directly for its target, twirling around in its perfect balance between weight and flight. Behind the arrow stood its launching point, the rusting iron bridge, offsetting it at an obtuse angle, the whole situ a discordance of geometry: nothing matched, nothing looked to be in place or how it should have looked. Everything seemed to be unfolding, tearing away from fixed points, as the short, stumpy arrow twirled, darting through the atmosphere, its kinetic energy heightened by the gravitational force pulling it down towards the swan's neck, where it hit the flesh violently. A sudden blow. Jamming halfway through its neck, just below its head.

For a moment there was nothing, absolute nothing. Silence. Everything seemed paralysed. Everything was unmoving and dead.

Then the swan erupted into a fit of agony, thrashing about hysterically, its enormous, full wingspan arched and flapping, its long neck flailing, bending and twisting to and fro, trying to remove itself from the pain. It suddenly tipped onto its left side, its whole head and neck submerged into the canal, hammering and wriggling like an eel out of water, helplessly trying to dislodge the arrow from its neck, hitting it, over and over again, upon the water's choppy surface. Then it began to spin around, frantically, like a canoe continually capsizing. Its mate was looking on helplessly, almost motionless except for a series of uneasy movements that consisted of straining her neck out towards him a couple of times, like she was in disbelief, stupefied by the manic scene that was unfolding before her. At one point the swan completely capsized, so it was upside down in the water, unable to regain itself. Blood was visible, covering the swan like bright paint, cartoon-like paint that didn't seem real.

It was the gaggle of Canada geese that had been paddling themselves up along the canal towards the bridge that made all the noise: a sonorous cacophony that seemed to overtake everything, each of the geese acting, as it were, as if it was each of them that had been hit by the stumpy arrow. The coots and the moorhens stayed far away, hardly recognising that something was fundamentally wrong. Least surprising of all were the assembled occupants of the whitewashed office block: not one solitary face peered from the line of looming windows, everyone inside completely unaware and utterly engrossed with whatever it was on their snazzy flat-screen monitors: emailing, checking spreadsheets, figures, project plans or on their phones talking about more figures, spreadsheets, emails, project plans, et cetera.

I didn't notice her rush past me; I was too transfixed by the violent spectacle happening before me. But then she entered the picture, standing on the bank, teetering over, reaching out to the flailing swan.

Before she jumped into the canal, she turned to cast a fleeting look at me. I cannot erase that look from my mind. But how many times have I said that? How many times have I commented on how she looked at me? All I know is that she looked at me and if I knew then what I know now I would have stopped her. I would have dragged her away from the canal, from everything. I would have stopped her.

She moved clumsily, awkwardly, like some weight had glued her to the spot, pulling her towards the canal bed, rendering any fluidity of movement an impossibility. She waded, messily, over to the dead swan. Reaching it, she made a final lunge, stretching with both arms out to grasp it, falling into the water, before resurfacing to hold it, the whole swan in its entirety, breast to breast. Then, struggling as before, she waded back with the swan, labouring to keep it out, above the water, back to where I was standing. She carried the swan in complete silence, steadfastly refusing to allow its limp neck and head to drag and loll through the water, straining and overly arching her back to lift it those crucial few millimetres above the choppy surface.

I shouted something to her. I cannot recall what it was, but it must have attracted her attention as she momentarily looked up at me again, just the once, to gauge her distance, as she made her way, slowly, back towards me on the towpath. The rain continued to bounce off her, sheets of it cutting into the murky water all about, trickling down the fattened breast of the swan. She proceeded with a blank stare, as if she was up to something ordinary, something she did every other day. It wasn't a cold look, as such, or without any emotion, yet it left me wondering if she was acting on sheer impulse rather than an intrinsic need to save the swan—but, as I've always thought, aren't all potentially life-saving decisions made on a whim, without caution, and therefore wholly mechanised?

My brother saved me once. Not from death exactly, but from a violent situation. I was in my early teens and had become fearful of almost everything. I was walking home from a friend's house in the area. The streets were busy and dark; it wasn't that late so it must have been in winter. I was walking down the Essex Road, and as I passed The Green Man pub, I noticed that I was being followed by three other lads. They were a little older than me, but not much. Pretty soon they caught up with me, after I crossed New North Road, when I was passing the row of shops set back from the Essex Road. Whilst trying to quicken my pace they stopped me. One of them pulled out a lock knife and held it to my stomach while the others rifled through my pockets and bag. I had nothing of any monetary value, or interest for that matter, on my person, so they began to indiscriminately kick me, laughing and shouting at me to keep walking. They continued to kick me, mostly in the shins and calves, trying to trip me up. I hopped and skipped, jumping out of the way. Then something hard and extremely painful hit me across both shins, which caused me to fall to the floor in immediate agony. I had been hit with an old wooden rounders bat. I was screaming in agony. I am, to this day, convinced that they were about to beat me into a pulp if it wasn't for the near miraculous appearance and intervention of my brother. He had been passing by on a Number 38 bus and had seen the attack. He had jumped off the back of the bus and dashed over the road to me and my three assailants, where he pulled me up from the ground and, without having to use any force or violence, made the attackers disperse, simply by naming the school they attended. On hearing this they walked away, swearing, grumbling, shouting at us both, leaving my brother to carry me home.

Years later, when my brother was drunk at a family Christmas party at an uncle's house, he—in the first and only time he had ever spoken about the attack—told me that it was a total fluke: he had guessed the school and had blurted out its name to them. Figuring that they were from the local area, and if he guessed their school correctly it might deter them. On the other hand, said my brother, in between gulps of the warm Guinness he was drinking, if he hadn't of guessed the correct name of their school, he'd probably have been attacked along with me, too. When he said this he smiled at me in a way that made me feel that I was his brother.

- seventeen -

She waded over to me in the rain, the swan hanging limply from her arms. Her clothes were sopping wet through and I could see the outline of her skeletal frame. Her hair was stuck to her face, water dripping down her cheeks. I inched closer to the edge. Again I turned to look up at the bridge, to see if they were there, to see if the Pack Crew were there, but they had gone. But I knew all too well who had committed this abomination. I knew instinctively that it was them. I knew it was the redheaded one who pulled the fatal trigger. I knew it was him. I turned back to her and held out my hand, but she ignored my gesture, slipping a little, but still moving towards me. Then she began to struggle, losing her footing a number of times and nearly collapsing into the murky water. I moved over again and offered her my hand one more time. Now the bridge was directly above us once more and we were finally shielded from the rain. She looked at my outstretched arm. I followed the trajectory of my outstretched arm towards her and the dead swan. Beyond her and the dead swan, to my right, was the lower floor of the whitewashed office block and the company esplanade. At first I thought I saw somebody there, staring at us both, but it was a large seagull resting on a hand rail, looking into the canal for discarded food. It opened its wings at full span, stretching them as one would an arm or a leg, one after the other, before rising up into the air, up above the canal and over us and the rusting iron bridge, cutting through the sheets of rain as if they were nonexistent. When it had disappeared from my line of vision I returned to my outstretched arm, holding it out for her. She waded closer and then struggled to free her right arm from holding on to the dead swan, letting it rest on her stomach and right thigh, her left arm still wrapped tightly around it, whilst she struggled to maintain her balance on the slippery bed of the canal. Slowly, she began to reach for my outstretched hand. I inched even closer to the edge, as close as I possibly could before gravity could grip hold and pull me off balance, aware of how unsafe under foot the banks of the towpath had become since the rain had started to pour.

Our fingers touched, ever so slightly, but she must have lost her footing again and slipped, as her hand fell away from mine. She soon regained her balance, determined to lift the swan out of the canal to what she thought was safety, all the while managing to keep the swan out of the water. She seemed unaware that it was dead. Eventually, she made one last lunge towards me: I gripped onto her cold hand, near squeezing out what little warmth was left in it, and guided her up towards me and the towpath beyond the bank's edge.

The more I think about what happened next the more absurd it all seems. It happened quickly, almost faster than time should allow for such things. In fact, it happened in almost no time at all. Yet each time I think about it, each time I run the events through my mind, knowing that in reality it happened so quickly, I purposely slow things down in order for her actions to reveal themselves to me. Bit by bit, slower and slower, frame by frame, until, finally, she is frozen there, in my mind, in time, unmoving, suspended. And then, just then, she is gone.

It is something I would never have predicted, yet she always knew that it would happen. She always knew, she had warned me about it, but I had never listened to her. I felt as if I had never truly listened to her. And if I truly think about it, *really truly think about it*, these events are a mere blip, a spot on a far horizon. Most people look back and think, where did all my time go? Why has my life passed me by so quickly? But not I. When I think back it feels like I had all the time in the world—whatever that means— and things have passed me by rather slowly. I have had a long life, and surely that's the point: for things to pass us by slowly? For time to drag? So that we feel we have lived longer? It baffles me why people are so obsessed with trying to fill this time with holidays, cars, designer clothes, technology, energetic sports, et cetera. Why would they want time to pass by quickly? Why would anyone want that? Those who bemoan the speedy passing of time at the end of their life are surely those same people who tried to fill it up with things to quicken its passing anyway, aren't they? Sometimes I don't know why I think about this anymore, but there is still one more thing that rankles deep within me: if I have had all of this time, if my life has passed me by slowly, with each day lingering pointlessly into the next, if it has really passed me by so slowly, as slowly as it now feels, then how come I never saw this coming? This is the thought that rankles deep within me now: how come I didn't see all this coming?

I don't understand, but I suppose there are certain things in my life, things that have happened to me, that I will never understand. Not that my life has been in any way exciting or eventful, or even interesting for that matter. Yet still, even these normal instances, these humdrum, everyday happenings that have galvanised over the years into something I can call my life, even these I cannot fathom. It's like I've never been born.

- eighteen -

I could feel her body weight, combined with the swan's, pulling back from me, back into the rain and the canal. So I pulled her, yanking her towards me, towards the bank, finally pulling her and the dead swan out of the murky water. She emerged and clambered up, steadying herself as she stepped up onto the bank, onto the cold, wet stone slabs of the bank, holding on to the dead swan. I let go of her, as

if we'd completed a natural balletic *pas de deux*, that she'd
landed, as if she was up on the bank completely, but she
wasn't, and as she tried to step towards me she slipped. Her
feet went from beneath her like she was on ice and she fell
sideways. I watched her fall all the way to one of the large
stone slabs that constituted the whole of the bank's edge, a
stone that had been there in its place for over one hundred
years. I watched her fall, sideways, to my left, still holding
onto the dead swan like its life depended on it. I watched as
her poor head hit the cold stone slab of the bank with ter-
rific force, cracking as she violently connected with it. The
sound of it, of her head, hit me in the pit of my stomach.
The dead swan landed upon her, its long neck stretched out
along her torso and down to her thighs, its breast resting
upon hers, wings limp and half outstretched, the stubby
arrow visible through its neck. The blood pouring from
its wound had already started to turn a deep crimson as it
began to oxygenate with the atmosphere around it. She lay
like this, the dead swan positioned suggestively upon her,
motionless. I was half expecting her to scramble back to her
feet, to jump up, but she didn't. I watched the dark, oozing
pool of thick blood—her blood—slowly form beneath her
head, covering the slab as it began to trickle back, behind
her, down into the murky water. Suddenly the dead swan's
neck jerked, momentarily caught in some nerve-spasm, and
then stiffen, before falling impotent and limp again, the
stubby arrowhead poking through the other side catching
on the stone slab beside her. She was dead, too.

She was dead. Her face slowly lost its colour and all
signs of the life that once possessed it. Her eyes were slightly
open; she looked dazed, ravaged even, staring into nothingness, unfixed and bleeding, blood shot and blank, her pupils
a dark blemish, blotting out any colour that could be possibly left in her iris. Her mouth, her lips were hanging slightly

ajar, as if she'd been about to open them to say something
before her fatal slip. Her whole head hung to one side rather
coquettishly, or as if she was embarrassed—if one can look
that way in death.

In death: she was dead before me, with her swan, its
long neck. Her left arm was still holding onto it, underneath
its open wings, clutching at its breast, her slender fingers
grasping between its feathers, smudged by its blood. It was
the way that the swan had positioned itself upon her that
left its mark: as if possessed by something, as if the image
before me there on the cold slab of stone by the canal was
meant to have been captured and scrutinised—by me, looking down upon them, in death, their death combined in the
perfect image. The delicate fingers of her free hand, poised,
as if conducting the final, delicate notes of a lost orches-
tra . . . the music fading, ending, the sonorous spectacle
fading into elegant silence. Her torso looked crumpled, resting on its side, the weight dissipating, her t-shirt, clothes,
clinging to her slight form, her midriff exposed to the wet,
cold elements, her dead skin pale and translucent.

I often think back to this moment, trying to capture
what it was—it seemed like I was standing there, looking,
simply looking, for far too much time. It was as if I played
no part in it, as if it had been meticulously acted out in front
of me, there beneath the rusting iron bridge, by the canal
and the whitewashed office block on the border of Hackney
and Islington, where each borough begins.

- nineteen -

I stood and stared at her blood, at her cracked head. Then I suddenly came to my senses and rushed over to her. She was lying on the cold slab of stone at the water's edge as if she was about to fall off it and back into the murky canal, the dead swan upon her breast. It seemed to be caressing her openly, the feathers fluttering in the strong breeze channelling beneath the bridge. I was frantically shouting for help, I must have been, I don't really know, it all seemed to be unreal. It is the image of her blood repeating within me: trickling onto the cold slab, sending me into uncontrollable fits and spasms, coupled with an overwhelming fear that had began to consume me. I began to shout her name. Over and over again, I don't know, at least that explains the noise that had enveloped me and the whole sorry scene below the bridge. The blood from the swan's neck had started to pour onto her thighs, soaking the flimsy, yet obviously expensive fabric of her trousers, mixing in with the rain, the murky water and the silt and mud, the gritty detritus of the canal smeared between each fibre. Her skin was still losing colour at a remarkable rate; she looked pallid, almost as if she was formed from a fusion of wax and transparent plastic. Her expressionless face looked set like the image in a poorly taken photograph—blurred around the edges, a little out of focus and over-exposed.

Her eyes were completely dead: two giant empty pools of nothingness, drained of all life and hope, of any sense that they may have opened at any given moment, and everything I had witnessed was some cruel, sick hoax played by my decaying mind. I could have dealt with it if that's all it was, if it meant her opening her dead eyes at that moment, to look at me, and then to ask me what had happened to her.

We soon attracted attention—a cyclist. He rushed over, throwing his bike down, and knelt down beside her. He checked her for certain things: breathing, pulse, wounds, et cetera. I asked him to leave her alone, to stop touching her, or the swan, and leave them be, to leave them alone together. He took out his mobile phone and asked me if I had called for help. I shrugged my shoulders helplessly, and he immediately began to shout at me angrily. He looked like he was going to throttle me, but he phoned through to the emergency services instead. He called for an ambulance, talking through her injuries and condition with the operator. Then he phoned through to the RSPB and asked them to come and collect the dead swan. Finally, he called the police. I stood there, motionless, above him, as he crouched down beside her. He kept on asking me, over and over again, what had happened, but I looked at her and the dead swan, repeating the same words.

"*It was them. It was them. It was them. It was them. It was them. It was them. It was them. It was them. It was them. It was them. It was them. It was them.*"

He began to yell at me again, although this time he was a little calmer in his approach, fatigued by my catatonic state. And then something strange happened: it suddenly stopped raining. As if somebody had switched off a shower in a bathroom, as suddenly as that. The rain simply stopped pouring so abruptly, it seemed almost biblical. I walked up to the opening of the walkway to Shepherdess Walk and leant against the new wall. I could feel the dampness of the rain soaking through the arm of my jacket now. And I knew right there, by Shepherdess Walk, what I had to do. It came to me in a flash.

From where I was leaning I could see up onto the bridge: it was empty and there was no sign that anyone, let alone a group of youths shooting at the swans with a crossbow, had been there at all. Everything up there looked calm and eerily quiet. Beyond the bridge and above the old warehouses in the distance, I could see the once thick, heavy clouds beginning to break, and light start to burst through them, great slanting beams of it cascading down to the earth, engulfing the gloom around them.

- twenty -

The police, RSPB, and ambulance crew all seemed to descend upon her and the swan at once. I watched it all happen: the swan carefully taken off her and lifted up into the white van parked on the Packington Estate. I watched them take her away, into the ambulance, her face covered. I eventually gave my statement to the police. They took me off to the police station near Old Street and asked me lots of awkward questions. They acted like they didn't believe me. I told them everything. When we had finished I asked them to give me a lift back to the canal. Then I walked back to the same spot where it had all happened. It had been cordoned off but I got as close to it as I could get by the rusting iron bridge and the canal, watching the coots and the Canada geese. The dead swan's mate was circling the spot where her mate had been hit, nonchalantly sifting the bed for food as if nothing had happened. Then, suddenly, it stopped doing what it was doing. As if it had just realised. It floated there, without moving, on the same spot where its mate had thrashed so violently. I watched her. She was beautiful. I stood watching her until she floated away, down the canal towards Wenlock Basin.

All the staff from the whitewashed office block had now dispersed from the company esplanade where they had eventually gathered to watch the whole scene with the ambulance crew, the RSPB, and the police unfold. I looked to see if I could see the man in the tight clothes and the woman, but they had gone, too. I wondered if they knew who the victim was. I wondered if they had realised it was the woman from the café who had accosted them earlier in the day. Maybe they would never know.

Maybe that's the best thing all around.

The rusting iron bridge had been cordoned off and a lone policeman was standing there, guarding the scene. He had told me to go home a number of times—but I didn't want to. He stood there. Acting on orders. Completing his task.

I was sure he was watching the coots, counting the Canada geese, and watching the murky water drift by him. He looked at his watch a number of times. Then he wrote something in his notepad before looking down to his feet and then checking the cordon a number of times; it seemed to be sagging in the middle. He strengthened the knots at each end, causing the cordon to become taut again. Then, as the clouds began to thicken the canal darkened. The murky water turned black like oil and a cold wind began to whip up its surface, causing ripples to intensify into a bubbling, choppy current of black goo that I thought looked quite beautiful in its own way. In the distance, up on the Packington Estate, I could hear a police siren rearing through the narrow streets. I guessed it was in pursuit of a stolen car as there were numerous screeches of tyres and grinding of gear boxes, then it began to fade as it left the estate. It began to fade. Everything began to fade.

I walked up a bit, past Shepherdess Walk, up towards the tree that I used to climb with the help from my brother. I took out my front door key and scratched her initials into the soft, wet bark. Then I walked home.

I was hungry. I had things to do.

- twenty-one -

I was raging. I wasn't thinking straight. I looked about, around my feet, in the nearest bushes, for something I could use: a stick or a brick. I picked up a short scaffolding pole from beside a contractor's skip. I held it in my hands, it was heavy enough to do some damage if needed. It was heavy enough to cause a serious facture, to smash teeth. To inflict serious damage.

I wanted to find them.

I wanted their mobile phone. They must have filmed the whole scene, the way they filmed the nonsense with the scooter. The way they knew no shame. They must have. I ran into the Packington Estate. The streets were empty. Silent. I wanted to find them. I gripped the pole tightly. I was ready to use it. I was ready to smash each and every one of them. I looked into every window I could, to see if they were there. I wanted to find them, to find that camera. I wanted to see it all happen again, to see it how they had seen it. I wanted to know exactly what they had filmed. I wanted to know, to see with my own eyes, if they had filmed her slip, her pathetic death. I wandered the streets, the scaffolding pole in my right hand. I walked into gardens thinking they may have been hiding, but I couldn't see them, I couldn't see anyone. It was as if the entire estate had vanished, just up and left for good.

I don't know how long I wandered there, looking for them. I don't know how long I held that scaffolding pole in my hands, convinced that I would use it. I don't even remember walking away, or giving up. I just wanted to smash them with the pole and get hold of their mobile phone, to see the events they had been filming, to see it all from their point of view. To pause the film where I wanted it to stop. To play it back and stop it just before the arrow hit its target. To fast forward past that moment, towards her, to catch her movement, to see her move again. To pause it on her face, as they had filmed her, to keep it paused in her beautiful face. Paused.

Eventually, I must have just dropped the pole by my feet and walked away, turned on my heels and left the estate.

- twenty-two -

It was during the summer holidays. At least I think it was; both my brother and myself were in the house all day long, which was quite unusual—the weather must have been bad that year, that's the only reason why I can think we were in the house together for so long. In fact, thinking back it most definitely was the summer holidays, as it was just after my brother's birthday, and his birthday fell just before the summer holidays started. Our parents had bought him an Atari home game console. I can't remember if this particular game console was the original model, *Pong*, the one that is now a collector's item; it might have been a later model. I remember being quite jealous of him, whichever model it was. I thought nothing of the game console's simple, two-dimensional graphics back then. In fact, despite that it was my brother's, I found the whole thing quite exciting.

My brother—who already had his own portable black-and-white TV set—had installed the game console up in his bedroom, pulling his bed over to the cabinet where his TV was placed, so he could lie directly in front of it whilst playing. We spent most of the day playing 'ping-pong', our favoured game on the console, competing against each other, game after game after game.

The small TV screen was predominantly black. The blackness was vertically divided-up into two equal halves, with a white line from the bottom to the top of the screen, where a crude scoreboard relayed the ongoing score to the players. Each half of the screen contained what I can only describe as a *bat*—each bat looked like an up-turned hyphen and nothing like an actual bat. Each could be manipulated vertically, up and down the screen in each of the designated halves, controlled by players via handsets. Each time the game began a white dot, no more than four large pixels, would appear in the player's half who was serving. Each player had to manoeuvre the bat to return the white dot, as one would return the ball in an actual game of ping-pong, back and forth, back and forth, until a mistimed return was made and the white dot was missed, the aim of course being to defeat the opponent by earning a higher score.

I suppose it was the sound of the game I enjoyed the most: a rather dull 'ping' each time the bat struck the white dot. After about ten minutes of playing, the clumsy mechanics of the game console were soon forgotten. My brother had become quite adept at this game—and, to be honest, I didn't mind the relentless defeats I suffered as a result. Sometimes he would become unnecessarily aggressive, though: shouting at me if I slowed down the game, or made a pathetic attempt at a passing shot. He would mutter things to himself, half sentences, little snippets, in varying degrees of anger and frustration:

"*Lucky bastard!*"
"*For fuck's sake!*"
"*If that happens again . . .*"
"*This control is fucked!*"
"*It's fucking fucked!*"

He got even angrier if he missed a shot, or if I scored a point, but I didn't care. The sheer enjoyment of that game was enough, its mesmerising acoustics, the white dot

travelling geometrically across the small, portable black-
and-white TV screen. I revelled in its simplicity.

Sometimes, when my brother was out of the house, I
would sneak into his room to play the game, setting it so I
could play the computer on a medium-paced level. I enjoyed
playing the game alone, knowing that if I were ever to be
caught I would be in serious trouble with my brother. Once,
after a marathon gaming spell, the bat seemed to stop of its
own accord. Like it had given up responding to my instruction or something. I lost control of the game all of a sudden, the bat sitting there in the blackness, unable to move,
flickering slightly, like there had been a malfunction, a short
fuse in the circuitry. Somehow, the white dot had become
caught, ricocheting off the bat and onto the parameter wall,
or the outer boundary, and back again onto the bat at high
speed. I watched this repetitive process before me on the
small TV screen, the *pinging* white dot surrounded by the
blackness. When I followed its trajectory, I noticed it was
following a perfect triangle, over and over again. I began
to feel strangely exhilarated, wondering if this was going to
continue forever on its own. I waited and waited, watching the triangular trajectory of the white dot, the blackness
engulfing it, outside it, within the trajectory, the dull *ping*
of the white dot hitting the bat, over and over, flooding the
entire room with its elementary timbre, pouring out from
the small speaker on the side of the TV. I stared at the
screen, mesmerised by what was happening before me. It
felt like technology, mathematics, this new stuff made with
computer chips and electricity fed into TV screens from
boxes covered in dials and switches, had taken control; as
if it was trying to tell me something, or give me a code to
decipher, in a perpetually triangular motion from bat to
wall and back again. I must have watched this phenomenon

for a good two hours. It must have been that long, before
I came to and switched off the game console, fearing my
brother's return.

Walking back to my room, across the small hallway,
I began to tingle all over, thinking about what I had witnessed: the triangular loop, the constant *pinging* in my ears,
the loop acting out its triangular trajectory ad infinitum. I
had never seen anything quite like it before that day.

The next time my brother left the house I waited until
he had walked up the street and out of my line of vision. I
watched him through my bedroom window, and when he
had vanished from my sight I dashed into his room to set up
his games console. But this time I didn't play the computer
at ping-pong. Instead, I purposely set the positioning of the
bat up towards the right-hand corner of the TV screen, as
best I could remember from my previous encounter of the
phenomenon. With the game in motion, and the computer
thinking that I was legitimately playing, I waited until the
white dot became trapped again, until it began ricocheting,
of its own accord, in an elongated figure eight this time,
bouncing from the bat, onto the opposing bat, down to a
wall, off that wall and onto the opposite wall, and then
crossing the screen and back onto the original bat—over
and over again, the *pinging* from the TV set filling, not the
blackness on the screen, but the space of my brother's room,
around me, around his things, everything. I must have left
it like this all afternoon. I can't begin to describe how right
it felt, watching the white dot's trajectory, feeling part of it,
knowing that it was never going to stop if I left it like that.

I can't begin to describe how that simple act of repeti-
tion back then made me so ecstatically happy—but it did. It
was probably the happiest I have ever been. The sad thing
about it is that I wasn't aware of it back then.

- twenty-three -

I didn't know what else to do, so I walked to the canal. It felt odd knowing that she was gone and that she would never turn up again. Even though she had been dead a number of weeks by then, it still hadn't properly hit me—although the weight of it all was evident in each of my deadened footfalls. The sun was shining above me and its rays were twinkling as they bounced off the canal. In the end, the dredger had done its job well. The canal looked cleaner now that things had settled—only the water remained; the silt and the shit had all but disappeared. The water looked calm. It looked peaceful, as if it had always looked like that, motionless and quite unaffected by things.

I walked towards the bridge, from the direction of where the bench used to be, where we used to sit, doing nothing every day, barely speaking, watching it all go by. I stood still for a moment and looked back. The recently erected wooden partition that separated the towpath from the newly forming concrete structures on the other side had been covered in graffiti. Some of it I could read: PACK CREW N1 spray-painted crudely a number of times across its surface, the markings of a territory, like cartographic markings on a map. The rest was meaningless to me, a jumble of elaborately formed letters, some coloured, others outlined or shaded in, all put there for someone to read, to see, to decipher—but not for me.

I looked up. A Beoing 747 was banking above me, well on its descent towards Heathrow. It banked quickly. It cut through some cloud, slicing it. It moved away from me at speed, far quicker than usual it seemed, straightening itself out and moving farther away from me. I watched it until I could see it no more. The whole scene lasting no longer than ten seconds. And then it was gone, and things were silent.

I turned back around and faced the bridge ahead of me, the whitewashed office block across the canal to my right. I stared at the bridge. It was the first time I had looked at it since it had happened. It was a simple bridge, hardly noticeable amongst the buildings that surrounded it. Even the canal beneath it seemed somehow detached. Yet, there it stood, connecting one side of the canal with the other, completing everything. The whitewashed office block was urging me to look over. I knew each of the office workers was inside, busying away at things—I also knew they would be there, sitting at their desks, sending each other their secret emails, waiting to sneak outside, or waiting to meet inside The Rheidol Rooms café at lunch. I tried not to look over, but the temptation was too much for me: I could clearly see each of the office workers sitting at their desks, or standing by the water cooler, chatting in groups, or on the phone. I observed them for a long time—observed their movements, scurrying about the office like lab rats on a task. I have never been able to understand the *things* of work. I've never been able to fathom why it has taken us so long to develop a system of existence that makes no sense to me. I really don't know if this is my failing or theirs, or whether I am somehow unhinged, or different—but the feeling is that I now know something, something blindingly obvious, something they can't see.

Before I reached Shepherdess Walk, where the path led up towards the bridge, I noticed the tree to my left. The same tree I had climbed as a child, the same tree I had scraped her initials into that wet afternoon with my front door key. The bark had hardened and lightened in colour where it had dried out in the sun. A lip had formed around the outline of her initials where the bark had begun the process of self-repair; her initials now looked like they could have been scraped into the bark years ago. The bark had dealt with the trauma, the cutting and chipping away with the key. I stood and looked at the initials, her initials, and smiled. Then I turned back to the spot where she fell with the swan, the dead swan in her arms, the life bleeding out from her fractured skull. I walked over to the exact spot by the side of the canal where her head had hit the cold, wet stone. I crouched down and traced my fingers where she had lay. I half expected to find something there, something she might have left behind for me, some trace of her *being* there. But the stone looked like all the others that lined the banks of the canal. There was nothing, no trace of her, no deposit for me to scrutinise . . . Nothing remained where she once lay to help denote the fact that some *thing* had happened there. I let my fingers trace the cold, textured surface of the stone one last time, but I wasn't really sure what I was looking for, so I quietly walked away. I was close to the water, close to the canal; I could smell it, feel its presence next to me. It was strange thinking about her. The things she said to me before she died. It was strange knowing that she no longer existed, knowing she was dead.

My bones felt as though they were creaking as I slouched over to Shepherdess Walk. I looked up towards the bridge, directly above me, I knew that I would have to confront the redheaded youth and his friends at some point, knowing that it was them, knowing that their actions had caused her death. I knew that I would have to face them one day. It's just that I wanted to put that moment off for the time being. I wanted things to settle before I had to go through all that. I knew, though, by walking to the bridge, that the moment was drawing closer.

I walked up the small, narrow path to Shepherdess Walk and turned right at the top onto the road that led to the bridge. Before it a barrier had been placed across the road

in order to block traffic. The barrier looked like it was new,
like it had been installed that week. The sign read:

Emergency access
DO NOT OBSTRUCT

I don't know why but I began to read the sign over and
over again, maybe six or seven times, as if I was hoping it
would change and say something else to me, before I walked
up onto the bridge and over the canal. Directly opposite me,
past the myriad office blocks, tower blocks, and cranes, I
could make out the top of the Gherkin in the city. I stopped
in the centre of the bridge. The canal ran directly below my
feet, maybe twelve or fifteen feet down, maybe less. To my
left I could see all the way up to the Gainsborough Studios.
I thought about the man and the woman arguing on the
balcony, wondering what they were up to. Beyond that I
could see the tower blocks of Hackney. To my right I could
see past Wenlock Basin, towards Islington and the tunnel.
I began to shiver, my leg shaking involuntarily; it was up
on the bridge that their actions triggered her death. I inched
forward towards the edge, where the rusting iron railings
sprouted up from the bridge, erected to stop people falling
over into the canal. I looked down onto the water and up
through the gap in the railings towards the new concrete
structures that were beginning to dominate the area. They
had started to resemble flats, and I could see the box-like
rooms forming, layer upon layer of living space, box upon
box. To the right of this, still looking through the rusting
iron railings, I could see a large sign that the construction
company or the developers had erected for the benefit of the
people passing by on the towpath. It faced the canal and the
whitewashed office block. It was thoughtfully positioned,

so that it could be viewed from every conceivable angle. The letters of the sign were green—again to denote environmental awareness and progress—set in a thick Helvetica or Arial:

REAL

I looked away. It seemed absurd. I looked down, towards the canal. It soon dawned on me that I was standing in the exact spot where they must have fired the fatal shots with the crossbow. I wanted to know where they were. I wanted to know what they felt, and what they were doing that exact moment. I wanted their mobile phone. I wanted to see it happen one more time. I couldn't rest until I had seen it happen one more time. It felt like I could have waited a lifetime for them to appear—up on the bridge, waiting to confront them.

The bridge was filthy. Litter clogged the gutter by the road. A sponge-like substance had formed over the grid, where stuff—old newspapers, cigarette dimps, and general matter—had gathered and morphed into one homogenous mass. A sponge-like substance had formed all around me. It seemed to absorb every sign of moisture within its vicinity, causing the trickle of water in the gutter to stop, to become caught, or trapped, and then slowly disappear, vanishing into the mush of sponge-like matter and debris, slowly but surely becoming erased from the surface of things. The canal was quiet. In the distance, to my right, over towards the Packington Estate, I could hear the shouts and boisterous yells of a gang of youths. It was probably them, up to something nefarious, sinister—a brand new day of activity, hoods up, the useless CCTV of the estate missing all their action. I looked at the rooftops of the old flats, soon to be dwarfed by the towering concrete structures that were forming at a staggering pace, designed in a minimalist office in Clerken-well, or some other part of the city, shutting out an old way of life from the canal and its environs. I looked down at the water: I could see all the way to the bottom, my new height giving me a clearer view through its depths. There were things down there on the bed—detritus left over from the dredger, bricks and manmade materials, plastic, computer parts, and machinery—but not as much as I thought there would be. Then, as some pigeons took flight from the con-crete esplanade of the whitewashed office block, down to my left, I caught sight of something in the water, floating, or just beneath the surface, sitting there, stationary, flicker-ing. At first I didn't know what it was, but as I was about to turn away to look into the whitewashed office block, or follow the trajectory of the pigeons as they arched upwards with tremendous ease, I noticed that what I was looking at was, in fact, me: my own reflection wavering in the water, floating on the canal's surface like some passing, unwanted and discarded product: a plastic bag, or some packaging. I concentrated on my image, my reflection, my face looking right back at me, into me, and for a short moment, until the sun shone back out from a passing cloud, obliterating my reflected image for good, I felt like I was floating too, or weightless, hovering above the canal, looking down on things. For that fleeting moment, not knowing what was going to happen next, gravity was nothing to me.

Acknowledgements

I would like to thank my editor and publisher Dennis Loy Johnson for looking beneath the surface and seeing the same things as I do—words cannot express how grateful I am for this; Kit Maude for the early edits and judicious, intelligent criticism—there's a drink awaiting you in the French House; Dr. Paolo Feraboli of the Department of Aeronautics and Astronautics at the University of Washington, for taking the time to answer my rather rudimentary questions; Mathew Coleman, for digging in and weathering the storm; Brian Rourke, my father, for unwavering support throughout my life. And finally, to Holly Ahern, my beautiful wife, for teaching me the important things in life—this book is for you.